THE WATCHERS

As part of our commitment to world literature, Ruminator Books is proud to offer the following additional titles in translation:

An Algerian Childhood:
A Collection of Autobiographical Narratives
    edited by Leïla Sebbar

The Belt
    by Ahmed Abodehman

The Last Summer of Reason
    by Tahar Djaout

The Watchers

A NOVEL BY

Tahar Djaout

TRANSLATED FROM THE FRENCH BY

Marjolijn de Jager

Ruminator Books
ST. PAUL, MINNESOTA

Copyright 2002 by Ruminator Books

Published by Ruminator Books
1648 Grand Avenue
St. Paul, Minnesota 55105
www.ruminator.com

First Ruminator Books printing 2002

Originally published as *Les Vigiles,*
copyright 1991 Éditions du Seuil, Paris

Dustjacket design by Wink
Book design by Wendy Holdman
Typesetting by Stanton Publication Services
St. Paul, Minnesota

Printed in the United States of America

10 9 8 7 6 5 4 3 2 1

Library of Congress Cataloging-in-Publication Data

Djaout, Tahar, 1954–1993
    [Vigiles. English]
    The watchers : a novel / by Tahar Djaout ; translated from the
French by Marjolijn de Jager.
        p.   cm.
    ISBN 1-886913-54-4 (alk. paper)
    I. De Jager, Marjolijn.   II. Title.
    PQ3989.2.D538 V5413 2002
    843'.914—dc2

2002006870

PART ONE

For years now the messengers of Morpheus have been ignoring old Menouar Ziada. He often imagines sliding into sleep, falling down the steps that lead to the subterranean world where consciousness dissolves. It is a state of healthful torpor in which he pictures himself smoothing the sheets, checking the softness of the pillows, and listening to sounds fade away that might otherwise spoil a blessed sleep. But it doesn't last. The old man comes back up to the surface. Confronted with reality, he stands dejected for a moment, and then his body begins to tremble. He is sure that the coffeepot, always within reach and in use until late in the day, has nothing to do with it. This nervous trembling comes from a place much deeper inside his body and his memory.

Still, the old man had enjoyed a privileged life for more than two decades. It was his luck to have chosen the right side, the side of "the just and the infallible," as he puts it, during the period of bloodshed that was to decide the country's fate. Once national sovereignty was attained, he could have prospered like the others in his camp, amassing creature comforts and material

goods he never would have dared imagine: an apartment, a place to do business, preferential treatment, and
the periodic waiving of retrictions. Even so, he had acquired accommodations and a substantial pension. He
had delighted in these with a clear conscience and without asking himself any questions, even if sometimes
during the night he was racked with a vague sense of remorse. It seemed to him that these miracles could not
be his forever and that the day would come when he
would be dispossessed again, and deservedly so.

It is true that his situation and that of his peers had
not failed to make others, who were rankled by all these
advantages, jealous. Were these agitators forgetting that
the now peaceful fighters, before obtaining all this prop-
erty, had risked their lives—that priceless commodity—
for the liberty and comfort of everyone? Those people
should show a little more decency and gratitude! As for
him, Menouar wisely decided to ignore the envious and
relish the fruits of this horn of plenty in tranquillity, a
state he sought to perfect. Until the day, that is, when
a ghastly recollection of that heroic and brutal period
sprang up from the depths of his memory, setting off a
dull ache whose origin had been jolted. The unspeakable nocturnal terror, from which thirty years earlier he
used to awaken bathed in sweat, trembling, or having

wet his pants, is creeping into his bones again, keeping him on the alert.

The army of occupation had just taken possession of the village, bringing fear and confusion along with its equipment—weapons, machines, and unfamiliar devices.

The soldiers pitched their tents and the next day began to set up camp, which took them almost a week. Then, their work completed, they rounded up the villagers. Menouar had just come back with his herd and was getting ready to have lunch when the order to assemble was given. He left his spoon in the dish of couscous with milk curd and rushed out, as did the others. It was a spring day. Fat, garrulous bumblebees were forming a squadron that would swoop from flower to flower. The sleepy air, the scent of plants, and the many musical sounds of insects normally would have caused people to doze off, but instead an intense fear was knotting their stomachs.

A soldier, who could only have been a leader, began to speak in a loud, authoritative, and unpleasantly hoarse voice that, despite the unfamiliar words, made it quite clear he had no consideration whatsoever for those he was addressing. His brutish and threatening assertions pierced the flesh and minds of the villagers like sharp blades. Uneasiness spread. The people would have given anything to be able to flee and put themselves out of the reach of this enemy who had pounced on them with no warning, thundering at them in some incomprehensible tongue, planning, no doubt, to annihilate them. But the possibility of flight did not exist. On one side the soldiers stood lined up; on the other a field sloped away, and a few yards from the group was a small dry-stone wall against which a hedge of cacti grew. They were trapped.

Only the simpleminded Moh Saïd, in his filthy gandoura and fez, tried to force his way out of the nightmarish circle. All of a sudden he broke away from the silent crowd and with a terrible shriek hurled himself forward to climb over the stone wall. But a burst of gunfire stopped him midway. Shaking like a leaf, a young soldier, caught off guard and terrified by Moh's scream, had pulled the trigger. The poor simpleton bounced off the wall and tumbled to the ground, struggling like a felled calf that senses the approaching knife. A huge, unidentifiable organ was showing through a rip in his blood-spattered gandoura. A cry of horror rang out from the crowd. Soon there was not a woman or child left in the square.

Menouar was standing there trembling and unable to breathe, his eyes bulging and his heart stuck in his throat. Even though he was more than thirty years old, this was the first time he had witnessed a violent death. The sight of a corpse was unbearable to him. Every time someone in the village died, Menouar would find a way to break the rule that people go and see the body before burial as a gesture of piety. Poor Moh was convulsing on the ground when another soldier, undoubtedly finding the spectacle intolerable, approached the victim and pointed a submachine gun at his head. He fired two shots, and the body shook in a final spasm. Menouar realized that his soaked pants were clinging to one of his legs.

All night long, he lay awake while a raging fever pounded him. A few days later, he left the village at nightfall to join the resistance, the "freedom fighters."

With great humility and in his innermost being, Menouar would always recognize that he had performed this act, not out of patriotic awareness (such concepts were to arise mostly after the war had been won), but out of the irrational fear the soldiers had inspired in him. Since he was not leaving any children behind, he had taken the plunge more readily.

Many years passed and the country went through numerous upheavals—new comforts and needs, new ways of being, of moving around, of consuming. And suddenly, three decades later, the ghost of Moh Saïd rises up before Menouar, and from deep in his guts the fear of being surprised and shot at. Paradoxically, he feels safer in the open air than inside a house. The stone wall Moh smashed into haunts him. Having space to flee is vital. He often thinks of his mother, an unimaginably distrustful woman who would never leave her house unlocked, not even her bedroom window, and who used to inspect every nook and cranny before she went to bed to make sure no burglar or criminal was hiding there. Not for anything did Menouar want to be surprised inside four walls. Once this obstacle is removed, he trusts his legs, his body's toughness, and his ability to dodge.

He does his utmost to stay out of the house as long as possible, to keep busy on the outside. During the day, he stands in front of his door, unceremoniously stopping passersby (true, he knows them all, more or less) and keeping them there with his chatting as long as he can. This little game goes on until dusk, when the semi-darkness makes any encounter suspect, and, in their hurry to get home, people no longer let themselves in for discussions. Besides, it is not a very busy street, and after a while no one is passing by anyway. Old Menouar Ziada nervously watches the hour approach when he himself will have to go inside.

As darkness advances, the last swifts retire. The houses are still vaguely outlined before disappearing into the night like sinking ships. One after the other, the clear sounds of day recede as more treacherous noises take over. Menouar lingers a bit, and like a hungry animal lying in wait, he listens to the faint sounds of the night, a procession of stifled cries, strategic movements, microscopic ambushes, or chaotic escapes. A world, similar and parallel to that of men, lies there and struggles for survival, weaving its intrigues and setting its traps.

A pleasant fear comes over Menouar, the obscure fear of his origins, the fear of his rural childhood nurtured on spirits and cases of possession. He allows it to penetrate him; it creeps into his blood vessels, beneficial and fresh. It illuminates his whole body, and he begins to quiver like an insect in love.

When, having delayed his incarceration as long as possible, the old man knows he is obliged to climb the steps to his bedroom, he resigns himself, dreaming of one day settling in the main shopping street known as the Galeries Nationales, with its clothing stores and vegetable market. There Menouar will never lack for people to talk to.

Before stretching out on his bed, he stares from the only window in his bedroom at the wide nocturnal sea and the moon, sailing like a phantom ship; with eyes and nostrils he explores the fields all around, where the scents of so many seasons have settled and intermingled. These sensations prolong his insomnia. The bed in which Menouar tosses and turns creaks until morning.

On the top floor his wife waits for him. But obviously she does not count for much in spite of forty years of shared life or, rather, of life lived side by side. She must have existed at some point in time, no doubt, but it is a very old story, a story of no importance. In any event, right now her presence arouses no more feeling in him than an old stool or a suitcase might. He is convinced that if she were to disappear one day he would not notice it until later, when it was time to eat and there was no meal. Besides, only the most obligatory words and the most basic gestures are exchanged with women. He doesn't know whether being childless has contributed to this indifference between them—at least on his part, because a woman's feelings matter little. No sensible man would have tolerated a sterile wife, and Menouar is no exception; he only began to accept the situation when he realized that the curse was his. He even wondered one day, simply to be argumentative, why women did not leave men who are sterile. He had come to the conclusion that it was undoubtedly because children were never seen to be descendants of women but only of men. A woman has no posterity.

For a long time they kept hoping. Three years. Five years. Twelve years even. In those days a deep and incomprehensible affection used to connect him to this woman who had opened her most intimate self to him, had revealed joy to him, the abundance of the body and

its satisfied repose. It was a period during which he was
convinced that, in spite of how it appeared, the men of
this country had a very large place in their heart for
women and that they even preferred their daughters to
their sons. His father-in-law used to visit them often,
coming from his village on an emaciated mule laden
with gifts and delicacies for the bride. When he left them
to go home, he would bestow endless advice and prayers
on Menouar, who accompanied him a short part of the
way. When they finally separated, the old man, urging
on the lazy nag whose spine jutted out like a long
knobby fishbone, would shout one last plea, "So long,
Menouar, take care of my little fledging!"

How the little fledgling has aged! She has grown into
a crabby old bird, cloistered in infirmity and silence.
She is no more than a dilapidated piece of furniture
amidst other furniture that won't be long in joining
the junk pile. Still, it can't be said that when Menouar
spends his days outside he is fleeing from her. He is actually only deserting the house itself, the vicelike grip of
the four walls in which he runs the risk of being trapped
without the possibility of sniffing the wind and bolting
without a backward glance.

In his youth, when he took his goats, sheep, and
donkeys to graze, Menouar had known unlimited protective space. The only obstacle to his gaze was a bare,
ochre-colored mountain that it would take him half a

day to reach. His country's regained independence as well as his status as a freedom fighter, which allowed him to settle near the capital, had at the same time torn him away from the pastures and rural odors of his childhood. Once the happiness of living close to the powerful, the wonders of tiled floors, electricity, and running water, had worn off, he felt like a caged animal, like a plant crushed between cement. He began feeling a painful need for shrubbery, a longing to watch chicks and lambs grow, to inhale the strong smells of the stable, a nostalgia for sheep giving birth, for wet billy goats. He also dreamed of a wood fire, of the deep, moist earth where leaves were decaying. He talked a great deal about the country and sometimes even went there. But visits were not enough for him; he would have liked to sink his roots there again, dig in as far as his waist, feel the buzz of insects and germination rise up in him, the quivering of crouched animals waiting to jump their prey or dart from predators. Detailed memories gnawed at him sometimes, miniature Edens tucked away in the honeycombs of reminiscence: partridge nests in the thickets, wind murmuring in the reeds, river eddies in times of flood, fires set for clearing, rock crevices where rainwater lingered, and sheep lazily chewing in the shade of an old olive tree. Menouar yearned for a few trees in particular—the fig, the ash, and the medlar. Sometimes he had an almost obsessive desire to crush the leaves

of an orange or lemon tree between his fingers just to
squeeze out the scent.

Menouar had surprised himself one day with the
thought that if he had to choose between paradise
and the possibility of reliving his childhood, he would
leap at the second alternative. More than all the promised delights of the hereafter, he would have preferred
herding his flock in the early evening quiet, inhaling
the smell of broom and rosemary through his eagerly
flaring nostrils, and jumping like a goat from rock to
rock.

He had hoped to find rest at last and, in the paradise
of urban conveniences, to feel the providential satisfaction that was not in his nature, but he never managed to
feel at home and take root in this unfriendly compost.
Lacking the ability to dig in with the bulk and confidence of an olive tree, he settled for residing there with
the frailty of a lichen. His impregnable roots, his sensitive foliage, the solidarity of his branches were always
stretching out toward his village, toward the region of
his birth. He followed everything that happened there
with interest, made contributions to the building of a
mosque or the construction of a road, kept up with mar-
riages and deaths, and with family quarrels. But he was
quite indifferent to what was happening right under his
nose, just outside his front door. He would have been
very much surprised had someone asked him one day to

participate in some neighborhood project even though he had been living there for twenty-five years.

One afternoon, while passing by the garbage dump near the Galeries Nationales, Messaoud Mezayer notices two chairs and a chest of drawers that are still usable. Sidi-Mebrouk is a wealthy suburb whose many buildings, grafted onto the perimeter of the former city center, hold mainly executives and the affluent. This provides Messaoud with a clientele that pays no attention to cost and offers other advantages as well—many repairable tools are discarded, pens and pencils are strewn every-where by the children of comfortable families, to the delight of the offspring of Messaoud, who consequently keeps their school bags filled at little expense. Not dar-ing to expose himself to mockery and risking disgrace by dragging around in broad daylight precious booty from the dump, Messaoud chooses to wait for sundown to act, having first considered the chance that another devotee of old stuff might have beat him to it.

He slips out of his house right after the eight o'clock television news. Nightfall comes early in the beginning of spring. Messaoud looks around and sees nobody on the straight road that leads to the dump. He already knows the exact place the cleaned and repaired furni-ture will occupy in his house, a home that has begun to resemble a bazaar because of the jumble of objects accumulated through its owner's frenzy for salvage. At the same time, though, he shudders at the thought that someone else might have gotten there ahead of him. He is busy speculating and pressing on to clear up the matter when a muffled voice calls out to him.

"'Evening, compatriot, are you coming back from the mosque?"

Once detached from the wall to which he seemed joined, Menouar Ziada stands out like a specter. His insomniac wanderings have taken him rather far from home. Annoyed by this unexpected apparition and in spite of this bit of bad luck, Messaoud must nonetheless willingly engage in conversation.

"I just wanted to get some fresh air. Spring is off to a warm start this year."

He picks up speed, followed on his heels by Menouar, who is breathing hard to keep up. Messaoud is concerned about his pieces of furniture; he sees them slyly abandoning their assigned spots in the shambles of his apartment. He feels like running to shake off his persecutor. The latter is holding his own, still huffing and puffing and constantly clearing his throat as if an important secret that will not be revealed were buried there. Suddenly he finds himself beneath the bright halo of the moon, and his hunched-over shadow, tall and spindly, stands out, his head a crown above the frail neck as if it had been set on top of a stake.

"Compatriot," Menouar manages to utter in an unsteady voice (a sign of fatigue or emotion perhaps?), "I don't think I'm wrong in telling you that some sinister event is threatening our city."

This time Messaoud almost forgets his furniture and listens closely: perhaps there will be something to gain or lose in this "event."

"Is your discovery too secret for me to know?"

Grasping his importance and the effect he is having on Messaoud, Menouar stops to catch his breath, forcing his companion to stop as well, and lets a long pause follow before he starts again.

"I've thought long and hard before mentioning this to you. I believe there's a threat hovering over us that must be averted as soon as possible. The country still needs us and our devotion. We liberated it from the chains of the occupying forces, and it is our duty to guard its tranquillity, even if we old and forgotten veterans have put aside our weapons and made room for others."

It has been a long time since Menouar brought up his combat past to Messaoud like this. In spite of a certain anxiety, Messaoud is totally exhilarated. He feels something like a breath of adventure come over him. Shaking but tense, he asks, "What is this all about?"

Menouar puffs out his chest, posturing like a hero of

few words. "They should certainly not think they can get rid of us just because our hair is white."

For Messaoud exasperation now takes over from curiosity. Scowling, he decides not to say anything else, nor does he hurry on, afraid he won't hear the precious disclosure.

His companion senses he can't make him wait any longer. He comes very close, and with his musty breath pants the vital information in his face: "You know the abandoned house next to the industrial woodworking shop? Yes, Rabah Talbi's place, which as you know is the envy of many civil servants and merchants even though the owner is still alive. Well, imagine this: for a solid week now the place has been occupied by dangerous conspirators! The light stays on almost all night long, and in the morning everything is silent and hidden again. I've been on the lookout for hours on end to find out who these alarming tenants are. There's no doubt the house has been taken over by professional subversives who know how to conceal their plans as well as their identity. We should expect a great disaster in our city sometime soon. I'm counting on you to keep this a secret; you're the first and only person I've told about it."

During his early days in the city's suburb, Menouar used to spend long hours with Messaoud, reminiscing

about the village where they spent their childhoods together; Messaoud had come to the capital to look for
work fifteen years before him. He was an outspoken,
quirky man. He had a small grocery store the likes
of which hardly exist anymore, a shop where almost
everything could be found—from clothing and shoes
to household utensils, cassettes, and school supplies.
Menouar sometimes wondered how he managed to ac-
quire such an eclectic inventory. But what was most
striking about Messaoud was his overwhelming greed,
which defied any subtlety and pretense, a candid greed
that left one breathless.

It was here in town, with its proximity to power, that
Menouar had discovered the other's avarice. In their
youth, he had not noticed it. True, nobody owned anything then, and so there hadn't been any particular attitude toward a wealth that was nonexistent. Everybody
in the village lived under the same sign—a precarious
sort of survival supported by a small plot of gritty land
and some goats or sheep the families owned in roughly
equal numbers. Those who made the impression of
being rich or "notable" could just barely saddle their
horse once a week to go to the neighboring market
from which they would return with some bakery bread
or factory-produced item. These expenditures made a
hole in their wallet that would sometimes not be filled
for months. At the time, Messaoud was just another

boy, which meant that the only thing he owned was a spare gandoura he wore on holidays.

Messaoud's grasping caused him at times to lapse into dishonesty. Determined not to lose anything, not to give up anything but, on the contrary, to whittle away at or win out over everything, the grocer had narrowly avoided just one form of excess, that of "making a mistake" in the change he gave his customers and thereby cheating the less watchful among them. But when he shopped in the Galeries Nationales he couldn't stop himself from taking price tags off products now and then or inverting the numbers, which occasionally gave rise to lengthy debates with the cashiers. When it came time to pay it was always entertaining to watch Messaoud make sure he had not dropped a coin or any other useful object. Moreover, every time he took something out of his pocket—his knife, his handkerchief, or, much less frequently, his wallet—his gaze would sweep the area around him.

In his anxiety to preserve and constantly enlarge his fortune, Messaoud, who knew how to write a little, already had a small notebook when he was very young. Here in imperfect spelling (though he was infallible when it came to numbers) he kept track of his possessions: 3 tops, 28 buttons, 35 marbles . . . His desire for customers appeared very early. Having come into a small unexpected fortune one day, he bought needles, pencils, candy, and pins from the village grocer, which he resold at a lower price in order to steal his clientele. It was the only time in his life that his ambitions were in conflict with his purse and caused him to record a serious deficit.

Strong coffee with a smell that penetrates like alcohol, a pipe exhaling aromatic tobacco smoke as well as a venerable past of tar and charred wood, an uneven pile of papers filled with writing and diagrams—Mahfoudh Lemdjad loves this intimate, enclosed world, these reassuring, stimulating, and familiar things.

For the ten days or so that he has been in this town, which he hasn't even had time to explore yet, he is content just to identify places and objects by their smells and sounds—trucks accelerating and roaring at regular hours, the horns of vegetable vans, motorcycles and old jalopies backfiring, hooligans yelling when schools let out, whiffs of dirty water or overripe fruit on the market stalls, the resin of city trees among which the eucalyptus dominates, and a nauseating odor indicating the proximity of a garbage dump. Sometimes in the evening, in the absolute silence of the closed-down little town, where you would hear the smallest footfall, a barely perceptible breeze brings persistent evidence of cooking or of the fields that aren't far away. Then Mahfoudh is willing to be distracted from his sheets of paper.

He releases himself from work and liberates his nerves, which start to relax. His body dozes deliciously, creeps through the luscious evening soaked in vague murmurs, and then evaporates. With a slight feeling of oppression, Mahfoudh is transported by this still unfamiliar town, unknown to him other than by its vapors and loud noises, its imperceptible ripples in which color and essence intermingle. He thinks of Samia, her invigorating laughter, her body whose memory pursues and torments him like an ache. Without his knowing why, the word *plenitude* comes to mind. A strong desire to call his friend has gripped him many times. But there is no telephone booth nearby.

How did he land in this unexpected haven? Everything began in a bar, the Scarab, through a combination of circumstances as happy as they were fortuitous. In a period of oppressive devoutness and numerous prohibitions, the capital city's bars (in some areas they had been closed altogether) remain among the rare places where one can have dispassionate and rewarding conversations. Mahfoudh is not one of those who spend all their money and energy there, who squander their potential in such a place and then go off reviling a castrating, not to say lethal, society. But sometimes he goes there, usually after a week of exhausting work. He has

ended up knowing the customs and some of the customers of the Scarab. Journalists (from the *Incorruptible Militant*, a daily paper, or the *Watchman*, a weekly)
go there to spew out curses and expound upon the
analyses they cannot put into print; filmmakers go there
to talk about the movies they are forbidden to make;
writers discuss the books they would produce if there
were the least little chance of getting them published. A
few teachers go there, too, scientists mostly, who are less
talkative and less demonstrative. Mahfoudh likes the
company of Hassan Bakli, a teacher of physics like himself, who has not worked for a while now—in order to
begin working again he will have to undergo linguistic
retraining, about which he doesn't seem too concerned.

That day as he walked in, Mahfoudh glanced at the
faces in search of his colleague, greeting some of the
people he knew in passing but not long enough to stop
and shake hands. Hassan was not there. Mahfoudh sat
down at a miraculously unoccupied table and decided
to wait for the possible arrival of his friend by ordering
a beer. Not feeling like conversing with someone he
didn't know, he congratulated himself on finding an
empty table and allowed himself to be overtaken by the
close atmosphere in which words, animated dialogue,
laughter, smoke, and the clatter of glasses created a kind
of formless and whirling jumble toward which he felt

himself drifting. He closed his eyes as if to facilitate the fumes rising to his head, opening his brain to the strange noises and images rapidly flocking there.

After his fourth beer he'd stopped thinking about Hassan. He was no longer waiting for anyone. He felt good all by himself. The noises around him seemed to have changed, both in intensity and character, becoming a thick swarm of indistinct sounds, uttered in every range and accent. The smoke, too, was transformed. Thick. At ground level. Drinkers were lowing, waving their arms around, then becoming detached like vaguely outlined, faltering puppets. Line and volume joined, rejoined, intersected. Mahfoudh began to find it extraordinary to be able to sit at a table alone in spite of the jolly atmosphere and pandemonium in which customers seemed to be sitting one on top of the other.

Then a gentleman, at least sixty or more, came hurrying over to him without even asking permission or apologizing for the imposition. He was well dressed, even if no razor had touched his cheeks in two or three days. He ordered two beers at the same time, gulped down half of the first one, then began a conversation with Mahfoudh that started off rather innocuously.

"It's a miracle they have started to sell alcohol again right after the religious holiday. Usually, the interval is longer ..."

"Yes, unfortunately our religion doesn't put up with

the joviality fermented juice doles out. We have several centuries of wasted good cheer to catch up with. That, no doubt, is why our citizens order two or three beers at a time, as you just did, thereby increasing their chances of reaching the level of indulgence and joyfulness centuries of severity have repressed."

Mahfoudh's companion began to laugh, showing several gold teeth. For Mahfoudh this was a sign of something he had suspected from the start, namely, that in spite of some neglect, his partner was obviously an affluent man. Besides, as the conversation continued Mahfoudh quickly learned the main points about him. He had a certain air of culture and was retired from a prestigious ministerial post. He had no children, but that didn't sadden him at all since it had enabled him to travel abroad and do whatever he wanted without any major restrictions.

In the course of the conversation, Rabah Talbi—as he was called—in turn learned some things about Mahfoudh, his profession, for example, the research he was doing to perfect a loom, and the difficult housing conditions that caused delays in the completion of his research. After these last disclosures, Rabah, looking preoccupied, remained silent for a good while. When he finally spoke again, it was to offer Mahfoudh the use of his house, some twenty kilometers from the city, where these past ten years he had gone only very rarely himself.

"It's right next to a woodworking shop," he added, "where you'll be able to get all the lumber you need to make your machine."

When they left the Scarab together that cool spring night, Mahfoudh found he had the promising solution to a problem that had long been plaguing him.

Suffused with silence and nocturnal fragrances, Mahfoudh tries to tear himself away from the enervating enchantment. He draws a long puff from his pipe, a kind of farewell to lethargy, and dives back into his pile of papers. He corrects a diagram, modifies an equation. The machine, truth be told, has much more to do with simple drawing than with theoretical research. The essential thing is to find the most aesthetic, the least cluttered, and the most functional model. What is left, then, is a simple computation of the dimensions, the resistance of the materials (wood and metal), the power of friction and the energy thus consumed, and the speed of rotation. But Mahfoudh enjoys stretching his work out, refining his design, checking and rechecking his formulas. For more than a week he has been living in a permanent state of elation. From morning until night every thought, every effort, every discovery is for the device being born. He is at one with this machine that is not yet, with this invention that won't qualify him as an inventor, for it does nothing more than perpetuate a practice that has existed since time immemorial, with which he is not really familiar but which seduced if not fascinated him from the first time he observed it as an adolescent, when he spent his spring vacations with his grandmother.

She was a high-powered woman who did not pass unnoticed in the village. She was the first person of her gender to own a purse at a time when women would hide their coins in a knotted handkerchief. She had also been the first woman to sport a wristwatch, a man's watch on a black leather band. An old devil in the village, famous for his smutty comments, had remarked one day in a small group (no relative of the person ridiculed was there) that she decked herself out with this article only so that men would ask her for the time and for more afterward, no doubt.

When the grandmother sat down behind her loom, she became truly exceptional. Mahfoudh, the child, would obsessively follow the up-and-down movements of the long wooden bars, while the rug grew longer and geometric patterns emerged as if by magic.

Some fifteen years later, when Mahfoudh went back to the village, he learned that looms had disappeared forever. Not one house had a loom or a grindstone any longer. The last person to own these tools of a bygone era, a somewhat unassuming farmer named Ali Blil, had remarried after the death of his wife, and his new spouse, who had big-city pretensions and whims, had done away with what she considered to be shameful and incriminating old things. That is how his loom had ended up in the garbage dump, together with terra-cotta crockery, wooden dishes, an old pestle shiny with age, and a rickety antique chest.

Mahfoudh had promised himself that by improving, lightening, and simplifying it, he would revive the instrument that for him would always evoke his grandmother's face and magical gestures. The idea had grown inside him for a good five years, sometimes taking over and sometimes fading away. It was like a nest of dreams that would change dimensions and outlines but never vanish. Then one day, he had picked up his notebook, and the majestic motions that used to make the yarn dance in earlier days began to guide him, to trace a line of clarity, secretly dictating the diagrams and equations to him.

Mahfoudh Lemdjad has spent the night in a state of great agitation. In the morning he can't even say whether he has slept or not. The local birds start their interminable racket.

So often charmed and stimulated by these persistent onlookers that spur him on in his work, Mahfoudh is almost oblivious to the serenade of his singing neighbors. His attention wanders elsewhere.

Clean and in perfect order, his file is there with a detailed description of the loom and a small-scale mockup. It is only ten minutes to seven. The government offices will not open for hours yet. Feverishly, but with carefully measured, slow gestures, Mahfoudh makes himself some strong coffee. He hears the spluttering of the espresso pot and lets it grow louder before he takes the pot off the stove. He feels electric waves run through his hands, irradiating his entire body. He pours himself a large cup and inhales its penetrating aroma. He takes a deep breath to calm the pounding of his blood and suddenly finds himself, with one ear, hearing the orchestra

in the branches. The out-of-tune serenade is beginning
to sound like a roar.

Time moves slowly in the sunny house. The coffee
and his pipe with its bouquet keep him busy for a moment, distracting him from his obsession. But it doesn't
last. Mahfoudh gets up, takes the file, skims a few pas-
sages of the text, and looks the diagrams over again. He
tells himself that the equations will undoubtedly seem
too complicated to the clerk who has the honor of opening the file. The bureaucrat will probably not understand very much, but Mahfoudh doesn't doubt that his
scientific formulas are going to kindle admiration and
respect.

Filled both with apprehension and optimism, his file
under his arm, Mahfoudh makes his way to the small
town hall he identified two days earlier. It has just
opened, but already a few early risers are waiting in front
of the windows. Mahfoudh's heart begins to settle down.
He almost forgets why he is there—or at least he has
succeeded in reducing his venture to less overwhelming
proportions.

He can't help thinking that, after all the angry pub-
licity against bureaucracy, government offices have become much more accessible than they used to be a few
years earlier. In fact, there was a time when it was well
nigh impossible to extricate a piece of paper or even any

information from the cranky organization. The officials at the windows would rudely dismiss any approach with "Not at this window" or "Come back tomorrow." To obtain any official document you would have to come armed with patience, calm, diplomacy, and sometimes considerable courage.

Things have changed, thank God! Mahfoudh knows that today he can count on them to be competent, affable to a degree, and have the know-how of a generation of efficient bureaucrats. He goes over to the window marked "Information" behind which sits an older man, well past sixty. Mahfoudh says to himself that he must be one of those veterans concurrently drawing a war pension and early retirement, while running a small business and holding down a sedentary job as well. He greets Mahfoudh with a grumble as if he is annoyed to have been interrupted in a vital and profound thought. He sullenly emerges from his speculative depths and looks long and hard at the younger man, though without any particular interest. What Mahfoudh says does not help, however.

Stressing each word, he recites his story: "It is a small machine, a simple loom. I have the file here with a full description and a model. Here, have a look. I'm applying for a patent. There are certain formalities I have to complete with your administration. I have been a resident of your community for only about two weeks and can't tell you how long I will be here. But it is here that I've put the finishing touches on my machine, and that's why I'd like the modest distinction of this invention to reflect on your town."

Mahfoudh has spoken without pause. The man at the window looks dazed and remains speechless, which causes the inventor to fear he can expect a disastrous verdict from this quasi judge. He puts the file under the man's nose together with the mock-up, which he lovingly unwraps. The old man is still in a fog and remains silent, his gaze empty. Suddenly he gets up and disappears.

It takes a while for him to return, and Mahfoudh is beginning to feel slightly anxious. For a moment the idea flits by that the problems of perfecting his machine will be nothing compared to the difficulties awaiting him in these offices and perhaps in the whole town. He scans the room and notices—is it an illusion?—that everyone is staring at him. Not just employees behind their windows, but also others who have come for their papers, are looking at him oddly. He feels undressed. His file and his laughable mock-up are hanging under his arm like irrefutable proof of his offense.

The veteran finally comes back and sits down without a glance at Mahfoudh, who feels obliged to open his mouth again. "May I see someone now?"

The other man seems to be coming out of an endless

meditation. He throws Mahfoudh a look like daggers that is meant to humiliate him, annihilate him, make him feel both his insignificance and his irrelevancy. At last he responds: "Your request is completely unusual and requires that our administration think it over. They ask that you come back later."

"When exactly?"

"Not long. Two or three days."

"What do you mean, two or three days? I thought it was a question of a few hours or maybe even minutes. I can't wait any longer than that."

When the other man continues to grant him the same attention as he would dromedary dung, Mahfoudh feels himself getting angry. Then something unexpected happens. The man at the window immediately drops his arrogant attitude, even tries to be communicative (which must cost him great effort) and mollify Mahfoudh. But it is too late. Employees have already left their posts to be entertained, and one man, whose appearance leads one to believe he has some authority, can be seen on the floor above, leaning over a wooden railing. He gives the order to have this nuisance sent upstairs.

Mahfoudh, boiling with rebellion and rage, climbs the staircase and finds himself facing the supervisor, who immediately tells him to come into his office.

"What do you want?" he asks without any introduction. He makes an effort to put on the forbidding look of a father about to reprimand his child but, fearing an unforeseen reaction, with no real intention of beating him. He is wearing a cheap suit, the pants of which have shrunk in the wash, and a slightly faded, awkwardly knotted tie. He doesn't know whether to threaten or to cajole. Faced with this unusual visitor, he is obviously disoriented, and his fidgeting fingers, with their dirty nails, betray his embarrassment.

"I'm here for a few formalities before applying for a patent. I've already explained all of this at the information window."

Following the example of the sixty-plus-year-old downstairs, this man, who is the secretary-general of the town hall, pauses thoughtfully. Then, in a wavering voice, both tired and resentful, he says, "It's not every day that we have inventors coming in. That's why you should understand our reaction. Surely you know that in our sacred religion the words *creation* and *invention* are sometimes condemned because they are perceived as heresy, a questioning of what exists already, that is to say, of the faith and the prevailing order. Our religion objects to creative people because of their ambition and their lack of humility; yes, it objects to them because its concern is to protect society from the torments that innovation brings. Besides, you know as well as I do

that we are a nation of frantic consumers now and of
practical jokers living from day to day. Schemers, yes,
there are those, and do-it-yourselfers who putter with
what is only imitation and of immediate use. But the
inventor—whom we associate with notions as bewildering as effort, patience, genius, disinterestedness—comes
within the realm of a race as yet unknown to us. You
come to disrupt our familiar landscape of men trying to
get war pensions, business subsidies, taxi licenses, plots
of land, and construction materials; who use all their
energy to track down unattainable products such as
butter, pineapples, dried vegetables, or tires. I ask you,
how do you want me to classify your invention in this
voracious universe? The best thing I can suggest to you
is to go home quietly in order to grant us time to reflect
and to allow us, if the Almighty deigns to help us, to
contain and digest our emotion. We are very honored
to be able to include men in our humble community
who work with their head instead of their stomach. But
I don't see why I should hide from you that you are
barking up the wrong tree and that you pose a serious
problem for us."

Mahfoudh doesn't remember how he got home or
what route he took. He is livid. He doesn't even think
of the very simple solution of working around this un-
pleasant town and going to the capital to take care of the
formalities. He does come up with the idea of driving

down there, but with the Scarab as his objective and not to confront some bureaucracy or other a second time. That would be too much in a single day.

He spends a few hours in a state of apathy, incapable of looking at his file and model, or even of picking up a book. The radio station is broadcasting songs that, when he comes out of his stupor, reach his ear every now and then. Suddenly he realizes the music has stopped and the news has come on. He turns the radio off and goes to the window. He finally stares at the panorama around him, which he had ignored these past days while he was so feverishly at work.

Just two decades ago, Sidi-Mebrouk would not have meant anything to Mahfoudh, although it is only eighteen kilometers from the capital, where he was born. At that time, Sidi-Mebrouk was a simple little town with a street furtively crossing it here and there, only to wander off again to places more worthy of interest, such as Rodania, Mekli, or Bordj-Ettoub. Sidi-Mebrouk then consisted primarily of a vineyard and orchards, a parcel of the immense and fertile plain that encircled the capital.

What remains from that tree-growing era is a tiny island of anemic greenery squeezed between houses. Orange and medlar trees, their bark scaly and covered with mildew, look on—Indians relegated to their reservations—while the tall white buildings and the impressive stores surrounding them nudge them over a little more every year, condemning them to an imminent death. Helplessly they see their enclosure shrink, cement skeletons replacing their uprooted or cut-down brothers. They watch the Galeries Nationales, just a few dozen yards away, a place of relative opulence and jostling that attracts a huge clientele from miles and miles around.

When the bus drivers arriving from Bordj-Ettoub or Rodania reach the stop at Sidi-Mebrouk they usually cry out, "The Galeries Nationales, everybody out!"

Sidi-Mebrouk has had an auspicious life. Everything began the day after independence with the establishment of a dynamic national construction company. Factories began to grow—a prefabricated sign factory, metal and wood furniture factories, and so on. Sidi-Mebrouk became an industrial zone. In a few years, its population more than tripled. Next to the well-kept houses predating independence (like the one Mahfoudh occupies), the place saw many private homes sprout like mushrooms, in addition to three large housing projects. But the count is far from over: elegant residences—small side-by-side ranch houses or two-story pagodas generated by the last sale of plots of land—display their unplastered bricks, the skeletons of their baroque towers, their spiral stairs. Nobody can tell where the subdivision will stop.

Mahfoudh looks at this profusion of money, cement, brick, and scrap iron, thinking that the region, so vulnerable to earthquakes, may one day shake its broad back like a whale and scatter and swallow up these temples of mediocrity that crystallize the aspirations of grocers. The shop is on the ground floor, the house above it on the second; sometimes it goes into a third floor waiting to grow still further. The insatiable desire for cement satisfies for only a few years: iron teeth always stand on the terrace in anticipation of the next floor they dream of adding.

On this perpetual construction site, in the excitement so favorable to business, commercial intuition sniffs the air and tries for the most profitable nooks: stores change character every few months, doctors' offices, maternity clinics, pharmacies, beauty salons, dry cleaners, and restaurants open up in the former "village" or on the ground floors of new buildings. Ambitious or merely realistic, some small merchants begin to reorganize their space to give it the dimensions and appearance a dynamic and prosperous city requires.

The peddler is as predatory as he is diplomatic. A born swindler who never runs out of arguments. Every time, he finds the flaw—even among the most hardened passersby—that lets him get to their wallet. He knows what buttons to push to make you show your money: he flatters the swaggering air of some, capitalizes on the good mood of others, raises his voice to the timid, and takes advantage of the foolishness of the conceited.

Messaoud Mezayer has fallen into the trap. He can't get over it: he thought he was immune to every plea that loosens purse strings! Most distressing is that he really doesn't even need the item the vendor has managed to palm off on him. He is worried sick, sweating bullets, and in a moment of distraction almost takes his money back from the trader's hand to flee as fast as his legs can carry him! But, even though he is infuriated, he has resigned himself. He, who never buys anything that he can't resell at twice the price, must be possessed, like the first idiot peasant that comes by. The more he looks at the fatal object the more he is convinced that no one will ever want it and that it isn't even worth cluttering up his store with. Unforgivable, a total loss for which remorse will pursue him for days if not weeks on end. What flightiness is he not capable of?

Messaoud wakes up dripping wet, his limbs stiff. Still incredulous, he looks around. It's just a bad dream. Thank God, he has purchased nothing! He hasn't allowed anyone to cheat him. Not a merchant in the world squeezed a penny out of him for some trinket. His money is quite safe in his wallet, just as he is under his blankets. He feels like crying out for joy, dancing pirouettes. He leaves his house exultantly, his soul weightless and sunny. He hums as he walks.

This morning, Skander Brik, the town hall's custodian, went to the homes of four veterans to inform them about the serious events of the day before.

Skander is a member of the informal police gathered around Si Abdenour Demik, a high officer with a great deal of influence. During the war of independence he served under his command, and nowadays it is his responsibility to report all facts and actions of any importance happening in the city. He executes this unassuming but steady work with uninterrupted zeal, and, beneath a most reserved exterior, his curiosity is always on the alert. Skander has made efficient strategy his second nature—he is like an insect with ultrasensitive antennae, barricaded inside his shell but keeping his senses vigilant like so many traps placed on the path of the careless. His gruff demeanor isn't conducive to making contacts, and certainly does not encourage familiarity or disclosures. That is a considerable inconvenience. But, aided and abetted by his apparent unimportance, Skander's talent for passing unnoticed offsets this. It is difficult to see an enemy in this insignificant and lethargic man.

The five veterans held a true war council at the house of Menouar Ziada. They attempted to evaluate the magnitude of the previous day's events, to locate the troublemaker on the chessboard of their enemies who are also the enemies of the official institutions, and consequently, of the country. They repeated the vow to struggle till their dying breath, never to let the flame of patriotism in them be snuffed out. The majority felt that it was most urgent to apprise Si Abdenour Demik of the situation; he would carry it to high places.

"But, while we're waiting, wouldn't it be right to bring the scoundrel under control?" one of the men suggested.

"Let's be cautious," another one said. "We can't act outside the law. It isn't up to us to supplant the forces of law and order, even if our cause is just."

"Yes," agreed Hadj Mokhtar, the spiritual, intellectual mind and theoretician of the group. "We must not let our patriotic conviction make outlaws of us, paradox of paradoxes. For, as all of you know, the law has never defended just causes—in fact, it has nothing to do with justice or truth. In peacetime people establish complicated processes, a whole chain of equivocations to legislate what is useless, to confuse the issue, and thus to allow the guilty who deserve punishment to slip through the net of outdated legislation. All that matters is not to lose sight of our Friday inventor, to tighten our surveillance. Nevertheless, we'll have to let him be free to move around, not make him suspicious in any way so that he himself will guide us to his ring."

The others pretended to understand everything he said, and the debate continued. The five partners declared themselves in favor of a method of discreet but constant struggle against this pernicious enemy. Obviously, the matter would be brought to the attention of the establishment (which must already be aware of it in view of where the incident took place), but they would not give up. They would always be there, watching from the shadows.

An indescribable crowd in the street known as the Galeries Nationales. The line is endless, the registers are being assaulted. A rare staple has just appeared on the shelves: butter, black pepper! Or perhaps they have just put sets of dishes on sale. Shortages can provoke great violence—for several days people have been talking about the attack on a truck carrying tires on the road that links the north and south of the country. The days that certain merchandise arrives in the supermarkets are horrifying times during which the Galeries Nationales resembles a ship when passengers are boarding. But these are the days Messaoud Mezayer is particularly fond of, for when chaos reigns he can more readily practice his petty thievery and other reprehensible acts.

He is actually in the food section busily changing price tags, putting the stickers from the quince jam (quite a bit cheaper) on jars of apricot jam, when Menouar Ziada grabs him by the shoulder. Messaoud jumps with fear, his heart beating wildly, thinking one of the security guards has caught him in the act. Even before turning around, his head goes into an accelerated and feverish deliberation that almost makes it explode. In a mere second he pictures several possible scenarios. The guard knows him and will only lecture him—some nasty fifteen minutes to live through. The guard will prove to be implacable and will stir up the overexcited crowd—an incomparable disgrace. The guard will act in a most professional manner—he will collar him and drag him to the security office. How will Messaoud extricate himself from each of these different situations? Perhaps, to save his honor, he'll go so far as to offer money to the guard for his silence. That would be a sacrifice from which he will not recover.

His lips show a pitiful half-smile when he recognizes his friend. It takes him a long time to suppress his agitation. But his relief quickly gives way to irritation—now he is forced to interrupt his activity.

The hubbub around them is deafening—cries of impatience, protest, or annoyance. Sometimes people come to blows.

Since the cash registers continue to be inaccessible, the two men prepare to leave the Galeries. Sweating and haggard, a young man emerges from a crush of people. Moving toward the exit and right past the two men, he says loudly, "If they put death up for sale people would buy it, too!"

Today Messaoud will not feast on apricot jam for the price of quince.

For a moment the two men walk on, exchanging thoughts on shortages and how impossible life has become, when Menouar stops, looks his companion straight in the eye, and says thoughtfully, "I wasn't mistaken. Rabah Talbi's house is definitely occupied by an individual with evil intentions. Yesterday morning he went and challenged our friend Skander Brik. And when they saw through his nefarious plans, he caused a scene at the town hall."

"Who is this conspirator, then? I thought I knew everyone in the village."

"He's not even from here! He's been sent here from who knows where by those who want to degrade our town."

"What exactly was he looking for? Did he mention his plans?" Messaoud asks.

"No. You know how people like that always present themselves under a false guise to infiltrate our institutions. Things would be quite easy if they admitted both their intentions and their identity."

"He didn't even give his name?"

"He introduces himself as a scientist who presumably has designed a machine."

"That sounds interesting. And what has he invented? A plane? A submarine? A refrigerator? A chemical weapon?"

"Nothing like that. You wouldn't believe me if I told you what he claims to have invented, the old joker—get ready for a shock, it's a loom!"

"Oh, no," Messaoud says.

He begins to think about his apricot jam and this untimely encounter. You'd think Menouar was born just to spoil his every opportunity to make a profit!

The two friends continue walking, and Messaoud, not wanting to prolong this discussion, uses the pretext of some urgent business to leave Menouar standing there—any discussion where nothing concrete is to be pocketed interests him only incidentally.

Menouar wonders if he was right to have provided Messaoud with this information. His fondness for his

childhood friend impels him to confide his moments of
worry, anxiety, loneliness, or—much less often—sense
of well-being to him. But their focus and their goals are
so very different, and, quite frankly, he doesn't know
whether he should really rely on him. Messaoud's greed
can carry him too far. Menouar is beginning to reprimand himself—will the secret he just revealed be kept?
Will the suspect not be alerted so that he can make different arrangements?

That evening at home he broods about all of this
and insomnia threatens. In fact, it is in the evening that
he lays bare his worries and tallies his setbacks. Nightfall, always accompanied by a feeling of defeat and
death, encourages this sort of brooding in him.

Some time has passed since Menouar went inside
and up to his bedroom. But he is listening to the breeze
in the trees and to the rasping sounds of the insects.
For twenty-five years Menouar has been listening to
these same songs—voiced by countless generations
taking over from each other so that the clamor will be
unbroken—and every time, along with the sounds, he is
besieged by the persistent scent of his beloved countryside, where each season disperses its aromas and pre-
pares magical ways of sending forth new growth. For a
while now he has been wanting to go back there forever
so that, before he dies, he can relive a kind of renewed
childhood surrounded by the smell of domestic animals

and the season's surprises. But deep down he knows that it is not childhood calling him but death. That is why he procrastinates, shies away, and delays answering the call. He invents excuses that are not without real merit—the suburb has its conveniences: the bakery, shops, electricity, and running water spare you from kneading dough, going to the market every week to stock up, collecting wood for the winter, and making the interminable trips back and forth between house and public fountain. Menouar has no children, and he knows that neither he nor his wife can handle these tasks—particularly not after a quarter of a century of urban life. (In reality, though, he is often under the impression that his life stopped the day he left his village and that everything he has gone through since then has been merely an accumulation of years in the anticipation of death.) Yes, indeed, he shall have to stay where he is, alas, until the end. Only then will he be able to resettle in the humus of childhood among the familiar plants and insects, in the cemetery overrun by shrubbery where as a child he used to set traps and look for partridge nests.

Menouar is thinking of the intruder who dares to threaten the tranquillity of the town. Deep down he is very proud to have been the first one to detect his presence in the city, to suspect some insidious plan while watching the house that stays lit up deep into the night.

Still, he recognizes that he wouldn't have taken the initiative to denounce or harass the troublemaker. He lacks the courage to take the first step. He would have thought twice before making any move that might entail complications, not to mention retaliations.

Had the intruder not exposed himself and fallen into the pitiless claws of Skander Brik, he wonders how his silent watch might have ended.

In the house in question, its light on this night as well, Mahfoudh Lemdjad is hardly giving any thought to the galling misadventure of the day before. But he can't concentrate. He just barely manages to fill the time by listening to music.

In the meantime, Mahfoudh focuses on organizing his thoughts and mastering the situation. Naturally, he panicked for a moment when he understood that the city's institutional wheels were going to break him, thereby permanently preserving their voracious obsessions. But he had gradually gotten a hold on himself and brought the incident back into proper perspective.

He would get a patent for his machine! He would even go, as he had intended all along, to the Inventors Fair in Heidelberg in two months. Suddenly he feels full of aspiration, prepared to tackle the struggle forced on him—there is no law that someone who revives a loom must be stoned to death!

He remembers the period in his life when he had to

go up against a great injustice, when he'd been caught in the devious and labyrinthine machine of the police and the bureaucracy. It was at the end of a student movement that had finished in a confrontation with the forces of law and order. Mahfoudh was not a leader. Nevertheless, he had been arrested with a few others and tried for "a breach of national security," then sentenced to a term in jail of which he, fortunately, had served only the minimum time. It had been a period during which absurdity, indifference, and contempt prevailed in an immutable system. Yesterday, after coming out of the town hall, he had the feeling he would have to confront all of that once more, would have to bang his head against the wall of the established order.

Luckily the music tears him away, lifts him up, and propels him toward another planet, to an ethereal setting that lasts only an instant. Then Mahfoudh is plunged back into the murky water of Sidi-Mebrouk with its sharks and their horrifying proximity. He really feels he is in deep, a solitary diver in a city where he knows no one, where his short and hardworking stay did not leave him any leisure time to make contacts or find people he might like. Now his decision is made— he will go to the capital the following day. He would have liked to see Samia, but their date is not until the beginning of next week. He'll settle for stopping by at his brother's and maybe finding a few friends there.

This idea calms him for a moment, bringing a lull in

the dark flow of his thoughts. He even feels overcome by secret delight, as if he were already far away from here, released from the quagmire. Excited, he takes a few steps—the simple decision has kindled renewed energy in him.

He goes to the window, leans on his elbow, and observes the countryside. Replete with threats, night is coming, but a creeping sweetness reigns as well. Slowly following the broad horizon first, Mahfoudh then looks down at the street. He is baffled—there are two people below about ten yards apart from each other: one is crouching beneath a bougainvillea; the other leans against the trunk of a eucalyptus tree. Disconcerted, Mahfoudh probes the darkness and then anxiety takes over—they are certainly not two people taking a walk.

He grabs the first weapon he sees—a metal curtain rod—and rushes downstairs.

The two figures have disappeared.

What do you like best, the little *d* or the big *D*?"

Redhouane, his eyes shimmering with intelligence, has just planted himself in front of his uncle, a character whose obvious and troubling originality the boy appreciates—he's thirty years old and he still doesn't have a wife! Redhouane has learned, furthermore, that his uncle does not pray—perhaps he doesn't even fast!

It should be added that the child has a strong and secret affection for his uncle; sure, it is a somewhat confused affection, for he cannot understand how such a wise and good man can wander beyond the confines of the straight and narrow! But with him you can at least have a serious conversation.

Mahfoudh gives up. That is when he learns that the little *d* stands for the devil and the big *D* for the Divine.

A whole code with religious keys like this one circulates in the schools, encouraged if not actually sparked by the teachers themselves. Although he is disappointed by these concerns that are so out of tune with childhood, Mahfoudh is nevertheless almost happy to be subjected to Redhouane's interrogations every time he comes to the house. At least they communicate, which is no longer the case with the little boy's father. Such boredom has entered the discussions of the two brothers that Mahfoudh wonders why he still goes there. No doubt because of a certain nostalgia for the time when Younès and he, in addition to their connection as brothers, were truly friends.

They were living in the old casbah, on the ground floor of a two-story Moorish house with a patio that overlooked a section of the city. It had minimal comforts—a single faucet in a corner of the patio, three separate bedrooms around the small courtyard, one of which was no more than a big alcove with no opening onto the outside other than the door; even during the day the electric light had to be kept on. But Mahfoudh has wonderful memories of this place, even though its reality was so oppressive. His is a selective recall that removes everything burdensome or ugly; all it preserves is the coolness of summers on the patio, the modern city with its thousand lights that the child discovered one evening while looking out from the terrace, the strolls and games in the dark, covered streets beneath the arcades and corbelled houses.

Mahfoudh used to love to explore the maze of streets and stairs that linked the sea to the hills in every direction. His brother and he were diligent students,

but they both also loved soccer and the beach. Mahfoudh had more of a tendency to live with his head in
the books, and it was Younès who would tear him away
from his papers and drag him to the beach as soon as the
summer turned really hot.

They would make some perfunctory preparations,
then take to the winding alleys, followed by the gentle
whiffs of summer and a slightly incongruous coolness
under the sweltering blue sky. Streets and stairs criss-
crossed at sharp angles. The street where they lived was
the longest one in the old city (it cut straight through
it). But that wasn't the right way to the sea, which is why
the two brothers would automatically thread their way
through a succession of narrow streets.

For them the trip to the beach was a ritual with its
definite odors and its anticipated "surprises," such as the
inevitable encounter with the vendor of lemonade fla-
vored with whole cloves. The sea breeze would whip
their faces as they came around the corner of a block of
low houses that looked out over endless stairs. They'd
stop, lean over a handrail, and breathe in the briny air.

Then Mahfoudh would begin to notice a different
smell—that of overheated asphalt. The city lay scorching in the sun, burning up in an invisible and savage
fire. It continued down below them but had a different
appearance there. The white buildings were posh and
separated by wide, tree-lined streets. Mahfoudh used

to dream of one day living there or in a similar area. When they crossed that wealthy zone, he would raise his eyes and look at the large balconies, where often a beautiful woman stood. On the way to the beach, Mahfoudh would carry this radiant and disconcerting image with him.

What also held his attention en route to the beach was the garden they had to go through. It was a kind of boundary garden, setting the old casbah apart from the more modern and affluent area. It separated two secondary schools as well, one of which was clearly more gentrified than the other. The Oasis Garden (Mahfoudh had always found this label, with its reference to the desert, odd) provided a break, a lull—as if for resting and dreaming—in the white plunge from the casbah down to the sea. After the flea market's oppressive activity, after the swarming and rather questionable area (haven't saintliness and poverty always been compatible?) of the mausoleum of the Sufi Sidi Abdelkader—where the devout, beggars, street hawkers, and matrons looking for mischief congregated— the rustling green space seemed both anachronistic and providential. It looked a bit unreal, almost suspect, because it was too beautiful for the panorama.

As they left the garden, it was only a few more steps before they reached the sea. Just above the beach there was a broad grassy embankment that dropped slowly toward the sand. It had shriveled bougainvillea, morning glories, and sunflowers growing wildly, all covered with a blanket of dust from the road. The crushing heat dehydrated the plants, squeezing out their aromatic sap, which would spread through the heavy air. The eyes and all the senses blurred, fogging over just a little under the palpable heat and before the soot-specked sea and the vast horizon of water, taut as an archer's bow.

Less committed to his studies than Mahfoudh, but perhaps also aware of his status as the older one who must bring money home as soon as possible, Younès at eighteen found a job in a bank. His relationship with his brother, a brilliant student in the science department, continued to be stamped with the same friendship. He married and had children without it diminishing or changing his attachment to Mahfoudh. Until the day when he, too, succumbed to the wind of godliness blowing across the land. Suddenly he became closed, wholly taken over by his prayers and his frequent visits to temples where he diligently followed sermons, commentaries on the Book, and theology lessons. He would still have discussions with Mahfoudh, but his tone was contemptuous and devoid of warmth. He did his utmost to push every conversation in the direction of faith.

Their friction had begun one day when Younès, who

was pensively observing his brother, suddenly spoke up: "You'd be perfect if only you'd pray."

Mahfoudh answered that such practices depended on free will and one's own conscience. For the moment he had no problem whatsoever in this area. His conscience was clear, requiring neither prayer nor piety. And besides, he had never claimed nor aspired to the perfection with which his brother wanted to credit him.

A long antagonistic debate ensued during which Younès displayed an unexpected passion and eloquence in defending the theses he hurled like absolute truths at Mahfoudh, thereby rejecting any discussion. Other equally stormy confrontations took place. In the beginning Mahfoudh thought that, over the years, grudges had built up in his brother and a sense of failure in the face of what was basically a life of mediocrity. He thought that in his religious devotion Younès was looking for spiritual compensation. For a short time, he even told himself that perhaps his brother was jealous of him because he had been so much luckier, at least professionally. Full of goodwill, he doubled his efforts to keep their former intimacy intact; he even had the illusion that he might be able to help Younès become reconciled to certain things.

But their ideas of the world had taken opposite directions. As Younès buried himself more and more in attitudes that brooked no reply, their communication became extremely painful before it stopped altogether. Younès did find the time to express vehement criticism of Mahfoudh's unmarried state, his relationship with a woman outside of wedlock, and of his not observing the religious decrees. Confronted with Mahfoudh's resistance and arguments, the fire of Younès's proselytizing died down and he was forced to give up. Since then there had been silence between them, evasion, insignificant exchanges—for fear that a new fight would erupt.

Now Mahfoudh notices to his horror that Younès's attitudes are affecting Redhouane. But he cannot tell exactly whether the influence comes from the boy's father or his school. After a religious faction instituted a series of reforms, the school has become a veritable military-religious institution—with the focus now on raising the flag, singing patriotic songs, and a heavy load of religious instruction. Rather than busying themselves with things that suit their age, pupils are preoccupied with good and evil, this world and the hereafter, divine reward and punishment, archangels and demons, heaven and hell. Mahfoudh has heard that some teachers occasionally practice moral blackmail on their students, forcing them to pray by threatening them with divine retribution, and even getting them to denounce parents who use alcohol. He was told about a school where every girl who wears the veil is sure to pass.

Mahfoudh likes to think that Redhouane hasn't yet become an informer. The confidence and openness in his eyes show he hasn't been irreparably infected yet. What prompts him to pester his uncle is without a doubt a desire to understand and instill a little order inside his own head, to clarify and organize certain values. For his uncle's example allows him to see that these "heathens" are not totally reprehensible. Some of them, at least, and Mahfoudh is one, are sociable, easy to talk to, generous, and intelligent.

Since Redhouane has calmed down, Mahfoudh wonders whether he should tell his brother about the snarls of the day before yesterday. He strongly doubts that Younès is really interested in what he's doing these days, but he tells himself that it would bring them a moment of serious discussion such as they have not enjoyed in a long time.

Comfortably seated in a dark, imitation leather easy chair, Younès, his head nodding ecstatically, is listening to a tape of sermons by a well-known imam. He is lambasting the powers and peoples of the Islamic world who are moving away from the prescribed path, succumbing to temptations and illusions with their sacrilegious glitter.

"I wonder," Mahfoudh says with irony, "if it isn't this heathen society that has put a spoke in my wheel."

"That would surprise me," Younès answers sarcastically. "This is your society, the unrestrained society that knows no moral order, the one you would like to see in charge. But what's the problem you're having?"

"You remember my talent for tinkering. Well, I've invented a small machine. I was going to apply for a patent, expecting to be congratulated, at the very least. But I ran headlong into a brick wall. I even think that the Sidi Mebrouk authorities suspect me of something and that they're having me watched."

"What do you mean, watched? I hope you're not suffering from paranoia."

"I assure you I caught some people spying on me."

"What can you expect from an unscrupulous police state that got where it is with the help of your ideas?"

"And the society run by religious law, which you hope to see in power, is that supposed to be more reliable and humane?"

"Religious law purges man of his lower instincts. It abolishes every difference, preaches honesty, respect for the other, and help for the weak."

"Aren't we rather running the risk of being carried back centuries in time and losing the values that people have created with their sweat and blood, such as democracy, sexual equality, individual freedom, freedom of expression, and religious freedom?"

"And you really believe that all these beautiful concepts you praise so highly are prevalent in that Western world you're so obsessed with? You think individual will is taken into account and women are respected there?"

The dialogue, becoming distorted, is about to go beyond jousting over ideas and turn into a shouting match when Leila, Younès's wife, comes to remind them that it's time for dinner. Mahfoudh goes to wash his hands, ending a debate he knows is going nowhere and in which it is very difficult to express ideas, given that the participants in the discussion are turning their backs on each other. Still, he does recognize that this time it was he who provoked the argument.

After they finish the meal he says good-bye to his brother, feeling once again, though more painfully each time, that their adolescence and camaraderie are dead, that Younès has relinquished all of life's passions and pain. Mahfoudh knows this society well, in which men struggle, have a good time, get their share of pleasure, and then when they reach a certain age—usually their fifties—turn a blind eye to yearnings and excitement. They cross over to life's other side, made up of disavowals and prayers, but undoubtedly, too, of nostalgia for the joys and indiscretions of their earlier days. What is terrifying about this new generation of zealots is their very denial of any pleasure, their refusal to accept differing opinions, their dream of subjugating the world to rigid dogma.

Mahfoudh is delighted to find Hassan Bakli at the Scarab. On the rather rickety table (the beer cap placed under

one of the legs must have shifted) are four dead bottles
that the waiter forgot to remove, as well as two saucers,
one containing green olives and the other with roasted
almonds. The racket surrounding them seems to origi-
nate from an ever-changing distance, enveloping them
or decreasing, creeping around at ground level before
dissolving altogether and making room for silence, a delicious vacuum interrupted only by the sound of glasses.
Then the shouting resumes, starting up the turmoil's
grindstone once more. Mahfoudh is studying the cloths
with their geometric designs that are attached to the
ceiling between the ugly plaster moldings and around
the huge orange plastic globe that covers the light bulb
like a makeshift chandelier. If Mahfoudh continues to
drink at this slow and almost contemplative pace, it will
be another two or three hours before spaces and objects
start tilting and his neck has to go into strange contor-
tions to restore the balance.

Hassan and he are silent. They don't need to talk.
Theirs is an old, intense, and bashful friendship. Their
roads have taken different directions. Hassan, who is a
few years older, did not complete his studies as easily or
steadily as Mahfoudh. When he was very young he was a
fireman, then a driller for a hydrocarbon company, before taking his exams and obtaining his university de-
grees. Hassan then became a teacher at the same school
as Mahfoudh, who, in addition to deep liking, feels the

kind of respect for him that an older and more experienced person deserves.

Mahfoudh would like to run into old Rabah Talbi as well. He would like to thank him for the house and to tell him about the machine—which, he feels sure, would please him. But the very instant he's thinking about Rabah and looking at the entrance, the character who appears there and then heads for their table is Nadjib Chébib. He is a large, bony man, a kind of thundering braggart who for the past fifteen years or more has been playing bit parts in films. He is tactlessness itself, and it is not without trepidation that Mahfoudh watches him approach, a broad smile cracking his mouth, his arms already wide open for an affectionate embrace.

He orders a beer before he even sits down and, becoming the only person worthy of interest in the hazy bar, captures everyone's attention, convinced they all know, like, and admire him. He starts talking about the film presently being shot in which he plays a war correspondent caught between his duty to inform and testify and the love for a woman who wants to get him away from the battle zone. But his story is frequently interrupted—he is constantly greeted both by clients sitting there and by those who are coming and going.

It takes only three beers, swallowed rather greedily, for Nadjib to release his oratorical energy, stretch his persona to the dimension of the pub, and become the star of a huge politico-aesthetic debate. Sitting at the other end of the bar, two of the speakers have become deeply involved in the discussion. Unable to participate from that distance over the heads and voices of the others, they choose to join Nadjib, which brings the number around the tippy table to five.

The conversation continues while the two make their way over, each with a glass and bottle in hand. One of the newcomers is wearing rimmed glasses and has a four- or five-day-old beard—one senses immediately this isn't neglect but rather one element of a carefully studied character whose other attributes are a stentorian voice, a specific way of drumming on the table, roomy and very elegant clothes, and making it a point of honor to contradict everything.

Mahfoudh and Hassan are not invited to speak, and the few times they try they quickly realize that it isn't easy and that the floor is only won by hard struggle. It is a game, or rather a test, in which Nadjib and the unshaven man do not readily tolerate competition.

The debate grows confused and ruthless, and Mahfoudh manages to understand that the point of departure is an article that Unshaven signed in the *Incorruptible Militant*. The smoke, the clinking of glasses, and the voices all around muddle the discussion, which Mahfoudh expects to turn into a brawl any moment now.

"The state doesn't need any geniuses, it needs servants," one of them says. (Mahfoudh cannot quite make out who, but no doubt it is Unshaven.)

"Unanimism is what drives me up the wall," a voice states hesitantly. (Now it is the third guy, Mahfoudh says to himself, the one who hasn't yet gotten a word in edgewise.)

"I really believe humanity doesn't deserve any better," another replies unreservedly. "What we should promote is an ethics of suicide. Teach people to take the plunge, to transcend this cowardliness that prevents them from fulfilling themselves in definitive nothingness."

"To cover up their cowardice they find refuge in religious restrictions—suicides are condemned because they dare to substitute themselves for God, who alone can dispose of life!" (The third fellow is making progress, Mahfoudh observes, for the one who just spoke again is the same one whose presence at this table was hard to understand only a few moments earlier, seeing that he was scarcely involved in a discussion that was starting to resemble a duel.)

"You're not going to tell me that those who've really made up their minds let religion or some other thing stand in their way at the crucial moment. And then, too, what a joke eternal damnation is! What our fellow citizens live daily, isn't that a form of damnation? I don't understand how they can hang on to a life they never stop complaining about. At every street corner you hear, 'To hell with this life.' Look at those fortunate countries where everyone is flourishing, almost too fulfilled, in any case with a hundred times fewer problems than we have here, and then look at the number of suicides there. While here, with this dog's life, the kind of existence people deplore and spit on, there is never a single suicide!"

The discussion is delving more and more deeply into metaphysical abysses—ideas and words ending in *ism* are bouncing off each other. Mahfoudh listens only intermittently, managing long stretches of reverie away from the verbal sparring. When he brings his attention back to the discussion, he notices that Nadjib and Unshaven have begun to compete not with arguments but with shouts. Ideas are being wielded like insults.

In the bar engulfed in smoke, raucous voices, and a profusion of bodies, Mahfoudh is lightly dozing. He suddenly thinks of his first hangover. He was eighteen. It was the year of his secondary school graduation. The preparation had been intense and inhuman. Molecular chemistry. Solid geometry. One day, deluged with practice exercises and reviewing, a friend and he decided to go and unwind in a bar. They each had four beers—he remembers the number clearly—out of sheer bravado, because neither of them wanted to be outdone by the other. Mahfoudh had no idea how he managed to get home. Once there, he hurried to bed and lay down. Then he started vomiting and talking incoherently. Beside herself, his mother rushed to his bedside, trying to identify the strange illness and already looking for the vinegar or some other old woman's remedy. That was when Younès showed up and smelled the alcohol.

"There's nothing wrong with him," he said to reassure his mother.

Then, bending over his brother, he said philosophically, "Mahfoudh, I've told you to stick to lemonade. Beer is much too strong for you."

It lessens Mahfoudh's tension considerably to see a solicitous former student at the window (he has to admit the young man wasn't one of the most brilliant ones, as he well remembers).

Confronting the administrative machine has always made Mahfoudh nervous. Contributing to this are the memory of an era when officials would send you packing at every step without further ado, of a kind of embarrassed empathy for paper pushers, and finally his recent bad luck at the Sidi-Mebrouk town hall. This is why the idea of having to renew his passport (he still wants to attend the international Inventors Fair, for which he has already registered) has made him anxious for several days now. And here, the morning he decides to confront danger at the assistant magistrate's window, he finds himself face to face with a former student, who calls out to him with a reassuring "Hey, teacher!" and offers his services to facilitate the process.

He begins by taking Mahfoudh out of the line and introducing him immediately to the person in charge of passports. The latter—with a mustache and a badly knotted tie that doesn't match the color of the suit he wears, not by choice, but because he must—receives them with the grim look of someone who wants to show his authority and wants to give the impression that he is not being forced, that everything he does is merely to be of service. He doesn't ask Mahfoudh to sit down, but, after the young clerk's plea on behalf of his former teacher, he proves to be efficient. He hands Mahfoudh his police record—a key element in applying for a passport, and the cause of major delays—in a sealed envelope addressed to the commissioner.

"If they are prepared to stamp your record on the spot," the department head tells him, "we will have your passport for you in a few days."

On his way to the police station, Mahfoudh reflects on the bizarre function he has been assigned—that of police messenger. It is the first time in his life he has been recommended to this authoritative body. He plans, upon arrival, to say with great self-assurance, "I'm here from the office of the assistant magistrate. The head of the passport service has sent me."

Mahfoudh doesn't doubt for a moment that the latter is esteemed by the police. Passports are coveted and slightly magical objects that citizens love to feel in their pocket, like a promise of escape. It's crazy, this desire to leave that haunts the men of this country. Going anywhere, as long as you can cross the border. To live the sweet liberty of the stateless in boisterous cities. Mahfoudh tells himself that nowhere else in the world can this feeling be known of being smothered at home, this desire to lift the anchor, to lengthen the distance between one's own country and oneself. Therefore, he is almost certain that the head of the aforementioned service must occasionally come to the aid of the police (as to all the country's bodies of authority) by putting a rush on the preparation of a passport for this or that protégé. Besides, almost every "head"—Mahfoudh's example is the principal of his school—has more or less visible contacts with the police. He remembers the words a journalist from the *Watchman* once uttered at the Scarab: "We should get to the point where journalists and the police each do their own work without interference and confusion."

At the station and at the sight of the letter, Mahfoudh is brought into an office with two police agents, one plainclothes man behind a typewriter and the other in uniform, busy filing documents. The uniformed officer takes the envelope, pulls the file out, and begins to staple the five photos of Mahfoudh to five different sheets of paper. The other officer, abandoning his work, types a form meant for the magistrate's office. The whole business seems to be going with unexpected speed. Since Mahfoudh has been personally recommended, the agents are taking him for someone important. Of course, the one handling the file would have preferred "company director" or "police officer" where it now reads "teacher." But why shouldn't there be three or four teachers in this country to have strings pulled, one of whom he has just encountered?

Before handing the signed report back to Mahfoudh, the uniformed officer has one last thought: "Go and take a quick look at the central file, anyway," he says to his colleague.

Mahfoudh suddenly feels himself losing his privileged status. He is becoming an anonymous citizen again, that is to say, liable to arbitrary powers, confronted with two all-powerful agents in a police station. Apprehension and doubt are beginning to overtake him—he's not going to get his passport. He remembers the abuse he suffered in another station when he was arrested twelve years ago, after the student demonstration. His last passport was refused five years ago for reasons that were never specified. He managed to obtain it only after some intervention. Why that refusal? Was it because of the student demonstration? Was it because of a petition he had signed on behalf of a cultural association? The signatories, having waited in vain for the approval by the agency in question, only later learned they had been documented by the police by way of a response. Mahfoudh hopes that the withholding of his passport is now a buried story—all the more so because it concerned an arbitrary retention with no legal basis whatsoever (other than perhaps the charge of "breach of national security," which was later dropped).

The plainclothes officer takes a few minutes to reappear. Even before he sits down again, he says to Mahfoudh, "Hey, you, you can go now."

"You don't speak that way to people you don't know," Mahfoudh answers icily. "But only a few minutes ago I thought I'd be going back to the magistrate's office with my report signed. You even typed the slip."

"That's what you think," the agent answers simply.

"That's what they told me at the other office, too."

"The magistrate's office does its job and we do ours."

"When will my report be sent?"

"Couldn't tell you."

"Did you find anything in the central file?"

"You can assume or believe anything you want."

Tired of the evasions, Mahfoudh gets up. He had great illusions about getting answers to such questions, and, when all is said and done, his partner in the game hasn't been all that awful, for policemen are meant to question and not to be questioned. It was only the "recommendation" from the magistrate's office that prevented the agent from being less polite, not to say harsh.

Mahfoudh's dream of being a protected and satisfied citizen has lasted about one hour and fifteen minutes.

He is trying to understand—have his "blunders" at Sidi-Mebrouk come to the attention of the police? Unless it was his peaceful student demonstrator past or his virtual association membership. Mahfoudh knows that one is always at the mercy of some unknown malicious cop who wants to put you into a central file where you run the risk of staying the rest of your life. He is, nevertheless, not astonished to have been treated this way, since a few days before, the Sidi-Mebrouk authorities had given him a foretaste of it (which had brought back other ones). In the end, he would have found it almost suspect had he passed through the normally tight net of bureaucracy and police. His failure puts things neatly in their place.

What bothers him is not to know the precise reason for the denial. But perhaps there is no denial; perhaps the police will actually return his report to the magistrate's office with a favorable recommendation after whatever verification is completed. Still, he is skeptical—the slip was drawn up in his presence and only after the central file was consulted did the situation suddenly fall apart. If they refuse him his passport today, he doesn't see why they should hand it over later on.

The Heidelberg Fair will be held in a month and a half. Mahfoudh is determined to move heaven and earth until that time to obtain his passport. The battle has already begun with the Sidi-Mebrouk town hall; he has gone through his baptism of fire and is no longer afraid. He is like those demonstrators who faced down the tanks; their fear is gone forever, for what they might have feared most has happened.

Three days later Mahfoudh goes back. His former student is still there, just as attentive as before. Once again he pulls Mahfoudh out of the line and brings him to the head of the department. He is still wearing the same suit (black, not very elegant, the suit of a civil servant in mourning) and the same badly knotted tie, but his attitude has changed. He throws the now groveling clerk an angry glance, and then, looking at Mahfoudh, whom he doesn't seem to recognize, he says sharply, "And you, what do you want?"

Mahfoudh reminds him of their interview three days before and asks whether the police returned his report.

"I've done everything I could for you, the rest is not up to me," the head of the department answers, then turns on his heels and leaves the office.

When Mahfoudh goes out of the office as well, the young clerk lowers his head, humiliated.

He doesn't know what to say, and Mahfoudh speaks up: "I appreciate what you've done. I'll wait a few more days. But I think that from now on you should let me stand in line like everyone else. Besides, we're all used to it. We know what waiting is. You shouldn't give me special treatment that might get you in trouble."

The boy protests weakly and mumbles that he'll still try to do everything he can to be helpful.

For the first time, Mahfoudh seriously sees the prospect of presenting his invention at the Heidelberg Fair disappear into thin air and it torments him.

Three days ago he was full of enthusiasm, ready to fight like a wronged man to obtain what was due him. In the refusal he saw only an anomaly that would be recognized as such; but the machine of administration and police now appears with a new face, indifferent, unmovable, all-powerful, and absurd.

He had already run into that. But he imagined that it was an accident, the exception and not the rule. Straight and endless hallways; silent walls that let no human sound filter through. For Mahfoudh the incarnation of this, of the labyrinthine maze, is one man. This man has a mustache, is insensitive and lacking in culture, wears a suit with no style and a crookedly knotted tie, and his nails are still black from some farmer's or shopkeeper's activity. The man without any personality or conviction is the one who seems to have combined all the criteria for promotion—starting at the lowest level, he moves up the ladder steadily and quickly because he will never be noticed, possessing neither the ideas nor the person-

ality that could bring thunder and lightning down on
his head.

An old colleague of Mahfoudh's, a philosophy
teacher, told him one day that during his long career he
had learned to be careful with the most mediocre and
most versatile of his peers, for he was convinced that
they were all destined to become important department heads, if not ministers of state. He went on to
mention several names among the highly placed with
whom he had rubbed shoulders but of whom his opinion was hardly flattering.

Mahfoudh waits another week before going back to the
magistrate's offices. When he arrives there early in the
afternoon (he has dressed in his most elegant suit, having decided to be impressive through his appearance),
he carefully avoids his former student, passing through
at the farthest possible distance from that window. Before going up to the second floor where the waiting
room is, he glances at him furtively and sees him bent
over his paperwork, his tongue sticking out a little as if
he were struggling with an exercise in physics or math.
He looks small and frail, mired in some bureaucratic
order he is perpetuating in spite of himself and that will
perhaps end up by swallowing him whole. Mahfoudh
wonders how the young man would react if they firmly
and definitely denied him his passport. Would he end

up pretending not to know him for fear of compromising himself—if he weren't compromised already? Would he end up suspecting that, beneath his respectable and intellectual exterior, his former teacher was perhaps just another criminal accused of some very serious things? Criminals come from every background, and those who are responsible for instructing and educating their peers are not in any way beyond temptation and reprehensible acts.

The staircase consists of just a few steps, and Mahfoudh very quickly finds himself in the waiting room. The man guarding the entrance doesn't allow just anyone in—first he asks why someone wants a hearing. Mahfoudh must have impressed him with his tasteful clothes, his pipe, his glasses, and his intellectual appearance (or maybe he looks like a political personality who permits himself the luxury of elegance and cultivation, something very rare?). He wasn't questioned before gaining access to the room, where only two people are patiently waiting.

After a two-hour wait, he is received not by the ministerial representative himself but by the secretary-general, who listens to him attentively and makes every effort to be of help. He goes so far as to phone the police station to ask for Mahfoudh's report, pleading an urgent mission abroad. Then he tells Mahfoudh that his report will be brought by a messenger who is on his way with other files.

Mahfoudh goes downstairs to wait on the ground floor, staying out of the line of vision of his former student. A few employees are watching him with a knowing look. Had he not just heard that his report was on the way, he would have thought his file had already come back with an unfavorable response from the police and that he was a suspect character.

The police station's messenger arrives, and Mahfoudh goes to the information window—his report is not there. Back in his corner, he waits again for another courier to arrive, until six-thirty when the magistrate's offices close. Since the employees have started to leave he was only barely able to avoid his former student by diving deep into his newspaper. But he is sure the young man saw him and, out of courtesy no doubt, didn't dare or want to come over to him.

Mahfoudh comes back two days later for news. Many reports did arrive the night before or early that morning, they tell him, but his was not among them.

Now he is convinced that he will not receive his passport.

The House of Adventure

The tall broken trunk. It was the child's hideout. And his laboratory.

But the books he had discovered a few months earlier should be mentioned first.

He already knew schoolbooks, both his and his brother's; he had seen comic strips with horses, Indian teepees, prairies, and mountainous landscapes. Then one day, he discovered—he doesn't remember how (did someone tell him perhaps?)—that books weren't only for instruction and entertainment, but opened a magic window onto the world and its panoply of adventures. That day a fever seized him. He suddenly felt an irrepressible and insatiable desire to discover adventures, charming people, scenic places, and perhaps exciting intrigues.

The first book that came into his hands, his first key to the unknown, was titled In the Tracks of Hunters *(Mahfoudh remembers the title precisely but not the owner of the book: was it his brother's or a friend's?).*

He also remembers that it was a day in early autumn. A fine rain (surely the first of the year) was falling in the patio, and a husky-sounding wind was grumbling listlessly through the alleys of the old city. Mahfoudh sat down on a stool in the covered part of the patio. He opened the book, impatient to enter the door of words into the house of adventure. First of all, he wondered whether he could read it all in one sitting. But he was too overcome and too nervous. The letters were dancing before his eyes, creating a mosaic of lines, dots, tiny arches, downstrokes, and tightly packed signs in orderly lines like a well-disciplined army. But no words, no adventures at all.

The child put the book down, did his utmost to control his emotion so that he could concentrate better. He closed his eyes a moment, and it seemed as if he could hear his blood beat more intensely as it circulated through his veins at increasing speed, then came pounding against his temples. Mahfoudh stayed like this for a few minutes, and then, deciding he had calmed down, he started the book again from the beginning. This time the project seemed far less taxing. Words were clearly delineated, lifting the veil off specific objects. But Mahfoudh was still impatient. He longed for the moment he would be immersed in adventure. He looked at the number of pages left to read and told himself that not only was he not going to finish the book that day, but he might never finish it at all.

The rain was still falling as quietly as before. Mahfoudh had stopped asking himself questions. He was traveling deep inside the book among the underbrush of letters and the fluid outlines of objects. He was in an uncertain world covered by a tenacious fog that would lift from time to time to reveal a defined square in the landscape, a tree sagging under snow, the piercing eyes of a wolf or a hut with a smoking chimney in the silent forest. Mahfoudh dug in deeply, sometimes stumbling or feeling his way in the half-light of a cold, white land among dogs and trappers tracking wild animals, in the discomfort of sleighs. He was handling objects randomly (only in his head, or with his hands? the borderline wasn't very clear) whose purposes were undefined, such as snowshoes, traps, and sleds.

Many times a landscape or a fantastic exploit put together with difficulty, word by word or letter by letter, would remain rudimentary, fleeting, or crumble in a stampede of frenzied letters. This crude decomposition of objects and places caused Mahfoudh a great deal of discomfort. Sometimes he would start the construction work over again; other times he would skip the obscure section and continue his exploration, promising himself to return to fill in the blanks later. The planet of words was enticing but so arduous and frustrating, too!

When Mahfoudh lifted his eyes off the pages dotted with signs, called back to reality by the wind howling through the narrow streets, his head was bubbling, shuffling bits of images, pure or hybrid items, and foreign-sounding words. He felt tired and happy. But a feeling of dissatisfaction gnawed at him. He expected better. He had only stood at the threshold of the house of adventure. He

had glanced inside, discovering specific objects and mysti-
fying tools. But he had not gone in. Unyielding words had
prevented him, had stolen the key from him each time and
thus hidden an essential part of the puzzle.

Mahfoudh again closed the book that kept a universe
of snowdrifts, wolves, pine trees, and blissfully heated huts
locked up inside its pages. It was evening. Mahfoudh ate
his dinner without looking at the plate, his mind roaming
over the snow-covered treetops. He reopened the book in
bed, and sleep overtook him in white spaces among the
raging packs of wolves and the sound of the wind rushing
through the dark streets of the sleeping old city.

It was the year in which he discovered books that the
desire to invent came to him while he was staying with his
grandmother. Vacation time always relegates books to the
realm of complete oblivion. Besides, there were no books
at his grandmother's. That was perhaps the reason why
Mahfoudh spent all his time outside in the fields where the
cicadas lived. Aliouate and Khaled embodied the great
revelation of friendship for him. They became his insepa-
rable companions. Both were his age but more solidly
built and swarthy from running in the scorching sun all
day long. He also found them both to be very ingenious.
Catapults, birdlime, cages, traps with springs—all these
paraphernalia they handled, and sometimes even fabri-
cated, with admirable ease.

The three boys combed the fields in search of adventure.

A house in ruins overrun by shrubbery served as their headquarters. There they held council each morning to decide on the exploits of the day, and from there they would launch their operations. That summer they had a very heavy agenda—birds to aim at, rabbits to track until dusk, fruit to steal in specific orchards, a river (actually just a mere trickle of water) to explore in order to find its spring. There was a kind of garbage dump (the children called it "the construction site") the three explorers would visit cautiously, attracted by a multitude of objects— mangled furniture, rusty, unusable tools, a whole array of bric-a-brac mixing metal, wood, and plastic.

There, the children one day found a broken scooter half buried under the rubble. They carefully dislodged it, cleaned it off, and tried to use it. But, besides the wheels, a good part of its handlebars was missing. It was really no more than a simple little board (totally wrecked) with a metal stick mounted on top. Nonetheless, the boys dragged it to their headquarters. They laid it down between the stones and the dwarfed shrubbery like a piece of booty or the corpse of a brave comrade.

They stayed silent for a moment, then Khaled suggested, "We should repair it."

"Or make another one just like it," Aliouate said quickly, as if the idea had already formed in his mind as they were transporting the ill-fated machine.

Silence fell again, heavy and smooth like a blade. In-

side his head Mahfoudh felt ideas and crazy subjects floating around and crashing against each other. Since he had
discovered books and especially since he had seen Aliouate
and Khaled handle traps, slingshots, and other devices (he
also had been watching his grandmother weave enchanting patterns and decorate ceramics), the fever to make
things had been gnawing at his head and hands. It seemed
to him that the moment had come to give his desire a
chance. Trembling inside, though it didn't show in his
voice, he said, "And what if we built a boat so that we
could go upstream and find the source of the river?"

That day the children stayed inside the shrubbery-
covered walls until late, talking about tools, materials,
and—for the first time that summer—money. They
didn't exclude the possibility of discovering a treasure
when they went upriver (as they now referred to the
trickle of water). When they headed back to the village it
was almost night.

They got to work the very next day. Of course, they first
had to put down various calculations and sketches on
paper, checked and corrected many times over.

In his grandmother's house Mahfoudh discovered a
tall broken trunk. He made this his hideout. And his laboratory. There he spent hours and hours creating the boat.
Did he have tools? Was he working with his hands or only
in his head? The coolness and half-light of the trunk were
favorable for cogitation. And for sustained work. Was there

no other reason for his choice of this unusual spot? Obviously, the invention had to be kept secret.

While working, the child often closed his eyes to cut himself off from his surroundings and to infuse himself better into the adventure. In the morning, harbors were very noisy. Mahfoudh recognized a few ships and crew members in the chaotic activity. He'd greet sailors in passing, call out to a docked boat. But he had no time to become involved in any discussion. Merchandise—some from very far away—was piling up on the wharf, and the men were loading and unloading without a moment's rest.

The child didn't know whether he should leave. He hadn't decided yet. It was only a question of time—he already knew the outcome of his hesitation. The wind of the open sea, laden with the unknown, pulled at him like a magnet. Still, something chained him to the land. What was it? Oh yes, he had to work at the construction site if he wanted the boat to take to the open sea one day.

They continued the project with delight, euphorically even. They didn't feel the tools' weight or the hardness of the materials or the grueling heat of the early afternoon. Night would come down on them unexpectedly, and regretfully they'd abandon the site, as a consolation already thinking about tomorrow's work. The site was in a state of constant animation; the boat was progressing fast. The cut trees were immediately lopped and subjected to ax and saw. The boards—whose wood still let off the smell of sap and live bark—were gathered, bent if needed, and tarred.

The prow was taking shape, defiant and adventurous. By its very longing it spoke of imminent departure. This kindled the children's energy and fervor, stirred their impatience to hoist the sails.

He had already decided that Khaled would be the boss. Sometimes, in the middle of grunts and groans, the sounds of the ax, the squeaking of the pulleys, Aliouate would raise his voice in a song celebrating the crossing:

> Traveler starling,
> Follow the ship's wake
> And ask my beloved
> Why she has run off.

The song was good for the children; it increased the strength in their arms and filled their heads with images. Mahfoudh dreamed—while cutting up the trunk of a poplar—of a slack and infinite sea with multicolored birds whirling above it whose bewitching song heralded opulent and perfumed lands. It seemed to him that it was toward these lands the diaphanous clouds were drifting, pursued by an obliging wind. He saw elfin colors dance on the mirror of the water. He never thought of that other, less hospitable sea, with its enormous white crests.

The decisive day arrived at last.

One after the other, the children put their feet on the brand-new cutter and, after checking the shrouds, they hoisted the sails, set the rudder, and under a favorable wind headed for lavish and adventurous lands.

Lying beside Samia, Mahfoudh is thinking of an endless beach with powdery, warm sand that invites naps and voluptuous stretching. He is not very talkative after making love and knows his silence is disturbing. He stuffs his pipe and Samia lights a cigarette. He finds the near ritual of smoking after their caresses a little ridiculous. But it has been like this for almost two years.

Usually, Samia and Mahfoudh are apart for about four or five days, then come together at Samia's only to separate again the next day or the one after. They don't ask for explanations, for news of the days they were not together, unless one or the other feels the need to talk without being questioned.

At this moment, drawing casually on his pipe and his mind visibly elsewhere, Mahfoudh feels such a need. The week just past has been filled with important episodes, and, except for the little bit he mentioned to his brother, he has opened up to no one. Who would listen to him more attentively than Samia?

"I've had quite an eventful week," he says between two puffs.

"A little fling?" Samia asks teasingly.

"Oh, no, much less exciting than that."

Then he tells about his disappointments, from the invention of the machine to the business with the passport. He feels Samia's heavy, unrestrained body against him, a delicate and sturdy planet. It has a magic power, is satisfying and soothing, and has the virtue of subduing anguish and loneliness. Mahfoudh relates his troubles, with the familiar and yet mysterious body close to his, taking away the bitterness and hateful twists and turns of his story. Tenderness wells up in him to the point of oppression. He is forced to move in response to the waves of arousal, to take a few puffs from his pipe. As long as she has known Mahfoudh, Samia has always been annoyed by one aspect of his temperament, though she hasn't dared discuss it with him—a detachment bordering on softness, passivity. A kind of absence without any cure.

"I think you should take a stand against such revolting practices," she says.

"They're trying to make people feel guilty, to plant the seeds of doubt in them. They want to force them to dig deep inside themselves until they discover or, if need be, even create mischief."

"And if you give up, they'll really think you feel guilty about something, and they will have found the flaw with which to confuse you. Then they'll have you in their grip because you've fallen for playing their game."

"What do you think I should do?"

"Write a letter of appeal."

"Yes, and if I'm lucky it'll end up on the desk of someone in charge. He'll straighten out the problem with my passport, and then he'll think he's become my benefactor and that I'm indebted to him the rest of my life. Especially if he calls me into his office, looks me in the eye with an overbearing, preachy, and pitying air, thereby presenting the face of a charitable man, of a father or brother to the rescue, depending on his age."

"It all depends on how you go about it, how you phrase the letter."

Before falling asleep, his body against the soothing harbor of Samia's, Mahfoudh glimpses the face of the chief commissioner, a huge man with a gap between his front teeth, whom he'd seen in his office at the police station the day he was there. At first sight, he didn't have that sullen and arrogant look of men responsible for maintaining order at any cost. Perhaps Mahfoudh should address the request, which he's already started formulating in his head, to him. But then he tells himself that, in the final analysis, it would be more efficient to direct it to an authority in the civil service. He decides to get the ball rolling immediately. It's the only way he'll have a chance of participating in the Heidelberg Fair. Clutching the prospect of a solution like a lifeline, he is almost reassured when he falls asleep.

In Samia's neighborhood, the morning is dull. It is nothing like the mornings in Sidi-Mebrouk, twittering and full of country smells. Still, this area is better than the one where Mahfoudh has his studio. The high walls of other buildings surround Samia's apartment on every side. Her vista is nothing but dirty facades covered with shutters and a very narrow crack onto the sea that looks like a piece of blue canvas, an open handkerchief in the distance.

And yet Mahfoudh likes this area and its calm. He has an irrational attraction for places like this. Like the old city where he was born. Like the wide shopping street of the capital where he used to walk around as an adolescent, admiring the sumptuous windows. Like the esplanade by the sea with its trees humming with the sound of birds in the evening, its fountain gushing from a stone, its newsstands where he would spend long moments of escape looking at books. Since he never bought anything, he was afraid of being noticed and so he spaced his visits—once (at the very most twice) a week. He also did his utmost, again in order not to attract attention, to go from one shop to another. This way he could delight in the maximum number of book covers without making himself unwelcome. Mahfoudh

promised himself he'd write one day, but he didn't know
what kind of books yet. He certainly didn't know how
to go about it.

Two of these newsstands have now been changed
into snack bars; the dream of the country's culture and
refinement has become stuck in an immense blowout,
drowned in a feast of the stomach. A country shaped
like a voracious mouth and an interminable gut, without any horizon or illusions.

Once he has finished his coffee, Mahfoudh is absorbed in writing the letter of appeal. He tries for a
general tone. Should he sound surprised? Indignant?
Conciliatory? What really matters is that he not beg, not
humiliate himself. It is late morning before the letter is
finally right.

Dear Sir,

*Wishing to participate in the Inventors' Fair to
be held in Heidelberg at the end of May, I needed
to request the renewal of my passport from your
administration. After going back and forth many
times—always followed by humiliating periods of
waiting—between the police station and your department (which even refused to provide me with
the special three-month passport, despite the explanations furnished), I must assume that my
passport is being withheld.*

Having never had any problem whatsoever with the courts nor with the police (other than one arrest and charge twelve years ago, later recognized as invalid), a step of this nature almost surprises me. I say almost, for my previous passport was also refused (again without any reason offered). It was necessary at the time to make use of "interventions" in order to have one prepared for me.

Since my conduct is absolutely beyond reproach, I refuse to resort to similar procedures on this occasion and to make the acquisition of an administrative document to which I have a perfect right appear like a privilege.

I vigorously protest against this bureaucratic and police obstruction. I would be most grateful to you, Sir, if you would be so kind as to look into this arbitrary and unconstitutional problem and put a stop to it once and for all.

Awaiting your kind answer, I am
Sincerely yours,

Then Mahfoudh contemplates the best way to send his letter. It seems better to avoid the mail, as anyone in the magistrate's offices could intercept the letter. He then decides to ask for an appointment with the gentleman and hand the request to him in person.

It is again the secretary-general who receives him

with the same guarded courtesy. "You still don't have your passport?" he asks with false surprise.

Mahfoudh is convinced the secretary-general knows the police have denied his request for a passport. He doesn't understand why the man is willing to stick his neck out by receiving him. He wasn't at all sure he would get this appointment when he asked for it. Perhaps the secretary-general has a nonconformist liking for intellectuals with glasses, while the system he serves mistrusts culture and intelligence like the plague. Yet, he himself is nothing like an intellectual. Perhaps, deep down, he wants revenge on a system that has managed to bring the most mediocre of citizens into its service; perhaps the system has actually made him suffer.

"I did not get my passport, and I believe I'm not anywhere close to getting it," Mahfoudh responds. "I won't go so far as to ask you for the reason for the denial. But you could do me a great favor by making sure this letter reaches the assistant magistrate."

The secretary-general grabs the open envelope.

"You may read it if you have the time," Mahfoudh says to him.

The secretary-general takes the letter out of the envelope and skims the content.

"I will make sure that it reaches him," he says, folding the letter and putting it back in the envelope.

Once outside, Mahfoudh feels a huge weight has

been taken off his back. He is happy. He had not expected to deliver the letter safely with such ease (for he doesn't for a moment doubt the secretary-general's good faith). He feels as if he is on the verge of taking revenge on what is unjust and arbitrary.

He strides off, his head stuffed with expectations that, for once, are not pessimistic. It is almost noon, and in spite of himself he is heading toward the faculty restaurant. For a moment he considered going to the Scarab to have a few glasses or mugs in the congenial group, in honor of what he, no doubt prematurely, already sees as a victory over police obstruction. But the Scarab is far away, and Mahfoudh is not at all sure that at this hour he'll find the people there he would like to see.

So he sits down in the faculty restaurant, glad to find a small table because he arrived early.

In fact, it isn't long before a line starts to form. Such lines always annoy Mahfoudh even if he himself has found a seat. It ruins his pleasure in relaxing, savoring a meal or a drink. He feels forced to rush.

He thinks of a reception given one day in a small restaurant after the defense of a thesis. Honorable doctors, contorted in their suits and suffocating in their ties, who only a few minutes earlier sat enthroned in the pantheon of ideas, principles, and theories, were stampeding to the buffet and unceremoniously elbowing each other. After a moment, the cramped room began to reek with an unbearable smell of sweat but, imperturbable, the scholars went on munching and guzzling in the steamy atmosphere.

Mahfoudh cannot manage to ignore the line, constantly watching it move. The spectacle of intelligence tumbling toward the stomach bothers him. He imagines food dropping from stomach to rectum. He then tells himself that these people, yearning for steak and french fries, might just as well lower their pants and begin to defecate right there, single file, discarding yesterday's steak to make room for today's. No matter how many record stores, newsstands, dry cleaners, and theaters have been changed into food shops these past few years, the lines never stop growing. You'd think they were feeding themselves through every orifice in order to stock up for a great famine. Or perhaps they are trying to catch up with a centuries-old hunger carried forward by a chain of ancestors who could never fill their bellies. Mahfoudh even wonders at times whether the people in this city know any other forms of hunger besides that of the stomach.

To take his mind off the horde of customers waiting for tables, Mahfoudh forces himself to think of the sea, so close by, but on which the city turns its back. He imagines it there, interminable and quivering, like a heaving chest behind the screen of buildings. A dream of departure moves inside him. He thinks of the Heidelberg Fair to be held in five weeks. Will he be able to participate? He has been corresponding with the organizers, and theoretically his presence is expected. He hopes the business with his passport will soon be resolved. Indifferently, he cuts the fish on his plate and wonders if it isn't actually what made him think of the sea—unless it is the picture window through which aquarium light is pouring into the restaurant.

He has finished his first beer and is thinking about ordering another when in the now much shorter line he notices a journalist from the *Incorruptible Militant* whom he has often seen at the Scarab. Just a chair to add to the small table and the journalist is sitting across from him. Now Mahfoudh is sure he'll order his second beer and maybe even a third or a fourth.

The newcomer starts to talk about all he has done to find a place to live—it's been going on for years. And Mahfoudh remembers that there is, indeed, a far more inaccessible and coveted item than a passport—a place to live. Besides, are the two—shelter and passport—not inextricably linked? Aren't people looking to run off to cities, if only for a few weeks, where they might at least find a hotel room in order to flee from overpopulated apartments, escape the displacement of forced wandering? Mahfoudh is contemplating this new form of dispossession—the impossibility of having a home, a private place of one's own.

"I have the same problem," he says. "I have a crummy little studio and no kitchen. It's almost impossible to work there, organize my papers. I first applied for a place to live about eleven years ago."

"That doesn't surprise me."

"Still, you can see what's being built, projects are going up everywhere, even on farmland."

"But," the journalist says, "the ones in power take it all—everything the country produces is for them. They must have apartments for themselves, for their children, their brothers, their nephews, their cousins, their in-laws, and their many mistresses. Since they've got enormous appetites and huge families, you can see the damage they do. But they don't only need family or bachelor apartments, they also need pharmacies, medical offices, research departments, beauty salons, pastry shops, and dry cleaners, not to mention the apartments they don't use themselves but make money on. So, you understand that the ordinary citizen without any financial backing, who applied for a place to live fifteen years ago, may very well have to wait another fifteen years and then die in the hope his grandchildren will be properly housed."

"To get back to something else, though still within

the realm of mistreatment, I've been having some serious difficulties lately and I'm wondering whether I might turn to your paper."

"What exactly is the problem?"

"I've invented a small machine I want to patent, and was first turned away, then trailed like a terrorist. Now they're even refusing to renew my passport."

"Withholding a passport is commonplace. It's one way the police use blackmail on some people. At the paper we get a lot of letters from citizens who've been victimized this way."

"I'd like to send you a letter that will, without a doubt, be quite harsh. You think it has a chance of being published?"

"It depends on whom or what you're implicating. You shouldn't touch power or those who represent it. Beyond that, go ahead. You can criticize every form of abuse, you can accuse anyone despicable as long as he isn't in power. You've already seen readers' letters about beatings in police stations or some minister's poor management or physical abuse in the prisons? The agencies of the state are sacred and therefore can't be criticized."

Now after the third beer and the journalist's rhetorical observations, Mahfoudh thinks again of the sea blocked by the huge buildings and of Samia's comforting body. Spring has settled on the city, but you can only guess at it from the brightness of the sky. To really see the spring, to feel and hear it through its plants and birds, you have to go up higher than the old city, to the lush suburb where posh villas nestle, hidden from the eyes and envy of others behind walls topped with shards of glass.

T he bird has flown the coop," Skander Brik says tersely to Menouar Ziada.

They are walking along the recently repaved sidewalk of the main street (across the street the sidewalk is full of potholes and in the cracks plants are doing their best to bloom). A wind full of hot, dirty sand has been buffeting the city for several hours. Fortunately, it is coming from far away and arrives exhausted, but it still manages to cover the sky, a pure blue this morning, with flaming red dust. All the smells of spring seem buried under this mournful blanket.

Without thinking, the two friends are heading for the Café of the Future. In the heat and dust there is nobody on the terrace. The customers are inside, where it is hotter, certainly, but where they're sheltered from the insidious, though barely visible cloud of powdery sand. Skander has taken over; he has chosen the café and now heads toward a far corner, followed by Menouar. He orders two coffees without even asking what his partner wants.

He takes a few sips before saying very softly, "Your

connection with the case of Mahfoudh Lemdjad (yes, the suspect's identity has been confirmed) isn't very clear to everyone."

"Other than watching the house from afar when the light was on, I have no connection."

"Why didn't you notify us? Perhaps if we'd caught wind of his intentions or at the very least of his existence, the culprit would have found us less helpless the day he made a scene in the town hall."

"I wasn't sure of anything yet. I'd discovered nothing other than that the light was on."

"What do you mean? In a house that's been abandoned for years suddenly the light is on night after night without anyone ever leaving it, and you don't find that's reason enough to arouse legitimate suspicions?"

"I've never been very quick. I've always tried to avoid acting too hastily, which can cause things to happen we may regret, as everyone knows."

"But the problem today is far more serious. As I told you, the bird has flown the coop. So, some people are wondering, and not without reason, whether he wasn't alerted by someone."

"You mean you suspect someone is in cahoots with him?"

"No, God forbid, I personally don't. We haven't gotten to that point yet."

Skander remains silent for a moment, a rare smile

across his face like a hideous scar. Menouar wonders if his companion would have allowed himself to smile had he not felt protected by the corner's darkness. There aren't very many people in the café, and Skander really could have spoken in less hushed tones.

Nevertheless, he starts the discussion again in the same furtive voice. "It's important to be more vigilant in the future. You know what role we have to play as first defenders and founders of the country."

Menouar feels like saying that the country belongs to all its citizens and that he doesn't always understand the mania of veterans to want to defend it against its own people. Besides, defend what exactly? The country or their own privileges? Does having liberated the nation give one the right to be so heavy a burden on it, to confiscate its riches as well as its future? But it would take much more courage than he possesses for that sort of utterance to clear the immeasurable distance between his thoughts and his tongue.

Menouar's silence goads Skander to continue: "You know our strength comes from our solidarity, from our concern to share equally both pleasures and disappointments, to act as one under all circumstances. Our relationships should be absolutely transparent. What will become of us if one brother begins to unnerve the other?"

When they separate in the street, crowded with

people despite the heat and dust, Skander's face (for the second time that day!) wears a strange smile, as hideous, enigmatic, and worrisome as the one he displayed earlier in the café.

Menouar feels overcome by an inexplicable uneasiness, which he tries to shake off by walking. He will go and look at the store windows, venture as far as the almost deserted Galeries Nationales where, in one area after another he can admire comforters, sports clothes, cans of paint, and a collection of axes in different sizes at his leisure.

In the evening in front of his door, he thinks of Skander's grimace, morbid and gleeful at the same time, a man whom he has never known to smile before. He tells himself he's beginning to stray, to worry for no reason, and that he's exaggerating the meaning of what the town hall's custodian told him. But as he turns the incident over and over in his mind, he cannot help but think of the war period, of one terrifying event. He remembers those days of indescribable suffering when he was almost and disgracefully killed at the hands of those in his camp.

The need to struggle in unison for a common ideal has never triumphed over devotion to one's clan and its grudges. One of the leaders of Menouar's underground group, a man of confident bearing and great physical courage, would sometimes display the same smile as Skander, and each time that smile came at a high price to someone. He nurtured an especially persistent hatred toward Menouar and seized every opportunity to do him harm. The day (or rather the night) that Menouar had joined the resistance, he expected to be received with the respect due to the brave. But the watchmen who spotted him first brought him to this commander, who subjected him to harsh interrogation, accusing him of being a spy, demanding details about his connection with the army of occupation, his patriotic beliefs, the reason he had come to the underground, and the nature of the actions he would be able to shoulder. Menouar, worn out with exhaustion and fear, taken aback by this reception and these unexpected questions, spent his time stammering and trembling—which reinforced the commander's hypothesis that he was dealing with a traitor.

That day, by he knew not what miracle, Menouar had escaped execution. But the commander's disapproval stayed with him. He and his immediate subordinates (affiliated with him not through rank but through a kind of clan pact) didn't miss a single opportunity to humiliate Menouar and make his life difficult. One evening, after the small group had met in a deadly clash with the army of occupation, the commander claimed they had been sold out. It so happened that two days

earlier Menouar Ziada and another resistance worker
had gone to a village in the region by mule to look for
fresh supplies. To the commander things were clear.
He had the two men tied up in spite of their protesta-
tions and pleas, and left them outside in the rain and
the cold (it was December) waiting to carry out a sentence known only to himself.

The accused were denied food and contact with
their companions. The first two nights, Menouar's body
consisted of nothing but pain. The cold scourged him.
Pain weighed on him like a millstone but spared his
mind. At the end of the third night, an unspeakable
hunger took possession of him. The terror of dying and
the agony radiating through him, with his solar plexus
as the central point, then became secondary. What primarily preoccupied him was the thought of eating until
he was full. All his strength had taken refuge in his desire to eat. If he could only prepare one good meal, he
would die without a murmur afterward, perhaps even
with his head held high like the hero he had never
dreamed of being.

He started to be delirious, to dream of lavish dishes
in which meats, sauces, vegetables, and fruits were as-
sembled with artful alchemy. He thought of dishes he
knew, but he did his best to imagine others both copi-
ous and outlandish. He had all the time in the world for
that. The cold that slipped into him like a knife, the rain

that drenched him, the rope that cut through his limbs had ended up becoming small, controllable pains, hiding in a remote part of his body, in a corner of his memory. His true suffering, his true delirium, had one name: eating.

For two days he didn't stop moaning, squealing like a piglet, imploring, pleading with soft words. He was making superhuman efforts to expel the pain hibernating inside him in a single cry. Then his body almost ceased tormenting him. He had reached the boundary where pain outstrips our strength and is transformed into unbridled exaltation. He was slowly and deliciously slipping toward a zone of annihilation and repose. He had just one moment of consciousness in which to realize that he was in the process of dying. Both dreadful and beneficent, a sensation came over him of being boneless, soft, and incapable of moving his limbs. His body was almost escaping from him; he was watching it (his own or that of his companion in adversity?) lying in the mud, inhumanly filthy, degraded, and wounded. A body waiting for the knife or for the end by starvation. As for the entity Menouar Ziada, it was a field devastated by inexorable want, monumental suffering that would only accept cohabitation with one other—starvation.

Perhaps it was the thirst he also felt that, suddenly, in spite of the rain and cold, made him think of a summer when he was an adolescent, a summer so torrid (he hadn't seen another like it since) that the domestic animals were dying and decomposing in a few hours. Maggots and flies proliferated on the carcasses. Lizards in unbelievable numbers were leaving their overheated shelters and coming into the houses searching for shade and water. Menouar saw them again trembling on their feet, their eyes staring, almost beseeching, their tongues hanging out, their chests heaving.

Then came a moment in which Menouar caught himself seeing the man responsible for his torment as a terrible and glorious father, with a devastating love, a kind of all-powerful god, master of life and death, a conqueror before whom the world bowed.

Menouar, who accepted the immutable order of preordained conquerors and conquered, would have liked to shower his torturer with words of submissive tenderness. A thirst for obedience poured into him from every direction. He would have liked to prostrate himself before the brutality of this man who was pulling screams and confessions out of him. Deep within himself, he knew that the tyrannical and adored father who was punishing him would not let him die. He believed in his love, his magnanimity, and in his omniscient fairness. He would have given anything to be able to shake or kiss the hands of the grand assassin whose scorn was like an ecstatic agony. He felt himself to be inside the skin of a vulnerable child who had been disobedient and was remorseful, who accepted being disciplined, who was ready even to caress the hand that punished him, ready for any sniveling and any show of affection, provided that he be set free. He wanted to feel his eager muscles again, attack the joys and pitfalls of the world with the vigor of his living body, pulsing with blood.

Menouar could not control the sounds that were coming from his mouth nor hear them once they were out. But he was certain he'd spent hours lavishing tender reproaches—as only mothers know how to find—upon the unflustered and serene commander, indifferent as a god who orders or shortens torture, and whose exterminating love is so dreadful to bear.

At the end of the fifth day another commander, more important than the unruffled torturer, arrived. After an argument with his colleague that almost turned into a brawl, he ordered the two victims set free; gaunt, starved, unconscious, shaggy, covered with mud, excrement, and shame, there was no longer anything human about them.

Three days later, the time it took for Menouar to regain the appearance of a man and be able to walk again, he was assigned to another sector.

The two men standing in the doorway look like salesmen or fortunetellers. Not seeing any reason to deal with either of these individuals, knowing he doesn't need to buy any miracle utensils or have his palm read, Mahfoudh is on the verge of closing the door when one of the unwelcome visitors says, "You are Mr. Mahfoudh Lemdjad, teacher at the technical high school, are you not?"

"Yes," Mahfoudh answers, puzzled.

"The commissioner of the fourth district wishes to see you."

Mahfoudh understands—two police inspectors. Once again he realizes how far the system in place is removed from anything elegant and beautiful; all those who are in its service act like horse dealers.

The two men throw inquisitive glances inside the studio. Without a doubt, they're looking for further clues for an investigation and would pay a stiff price to be able to get in. But Mahfoudh is there, blocking the door. Had they invited themselves in he would have prevented them from entering given that they haven't

produced a warrant. A few days earlier a vegetable vendor in the neighborhood told him: "Two men asked me
for your address. Since they were hardly reputable characters, I told them I didn't know you."

"The commissioner wants to see me right away?"
Mahfoudh asks.

"Shall we say this morning, preferably," one of them
answers.

Mahfoudh shuts the door in their faces and gets
dressed. Looking out of the window onto the narrow
street, he sees the two policemen below in front of the
building. He, too, goes down and follows them to the
end of the street, where they stop at a Peugeot station
wagon. All three of them get in the car.

Mahfoudh is not afraid, but he does feel very ill at
ease. He doesn't know whether he should talk or not.
Being on friendly terms with the police is of absolutely
no interest to him, and the silence seems like a fortress
of safety and dignity between these people and himself.
Yet, he wonders if he shouldn't ask for some explanation. Fortunately, the police station isn't very far.

One of the officers is the first to break the silence:
"We thought you were living in Sidi-Mebrouk."

Things couldn't be more obvious, Mahfoudh tells
himself, and answers the policeman, "I was born in the
capital and have always lived there."

These are the only words they exchange. But

Mahfoudh already has the information about the source of his trouble.

Preceded by his two guides, he enters the station where he had come four weeks before, self-assured, a letter from the magistrate's office in his hand. In passing, he glimpses the commissioner with the space between his teeth bent over paperwork in his office.

The two men take Mahfoudh, who had expected to enter this office, into a dark, cramped room instead, where someone is sitting behind a huge typewriter, as has not been seen in some fifteen years. Do those old things really work? Perhaps the whole scene is a sham, rehearsed for God knows what mysterious reason, in which this square-headed man with the build of a woodcutter will pointlessly start to tap away at the keys. He turns around to ask his two guides something, but they have disappeared. He is alone with the square man, who must have the eyes of an owl from having lived (and typed?) in the semidark.

Mahfoudh observes him carefully, assessing him as if he were the one about to do the questioning and not the other way around. The seated man shows no emotion.

Mahfoudh is beginning to feel afraid. Obviously, this man is built to beat people up, not to tinker with a keyboard. Devoid of any apparent intelligence, he resembles a veritable punching machine. Mahfoudh would like to see his fingers. He doesn't doubt that he

could tell with complete certainty whether they are ac-
customed to typing reports or extracting confessions.

He arbitrarily leans toward the second guess. He
imagines that those brought to this enigma behind a
desk are accused of every sin, every crime, and intro-
duced as the worst enemies of the country, God, and
honest people. They close the door behind the poor
victims, entrusted to this man for sentencing, and the
sphinx with the woodcutter's build starts to tear them
to pieces like a tiger.

Finally the man speaks in a neutral voice but one
that allows no rejoinder.

"Sit," he says to Mahfoudh, pointing to the old chair
in front of him.

This time Mahfoudh makes no comment about the
rude informality. He even tells himself he'll be lucky if
he manages to come through with nothing worse than
this benign lack of worldly manners. The man begins to
grill him, and Mahfoudh has to respond quickly and
concisely; a gesture of the hand (never a word) stops
him every time he tries to elaborate or explain. The man
taps the machine between barked questions. Mahfoudh
realizes that some questions are asked two and even
three times, and he wonders if the interrogator is mock-
ing him or checking to see whether his memory and
the veracity of what he says are faulty. Unless the er-
satz woodcutter is simply retarded. For Mahfoudh notes

that the repeated questions are those where the risk of a mistake is practically nil.

Mahfoudh has to respond to the following (some questions indicate knowledge he would have never suspected on the part of the interrogator):

His name.

His date of birth.

His address.

His level of education.

His activities during the war of independence.

Is his nationality by birth or acquired?

Does he know people in the opposition?

How many times has he been imprisoned and for what reasons?

His date of birth.

Does he smoke?

Does he drink alcohol?

Does he have homosexual or perverse tendencies?

His activities during the war of independence.

Has he read the country's constitution and how many times?

Does he think the justice rendered in the country is irreproachable?

Is his nationality by birth or acquired?

Is *The Prophet* by Khalil Gibran a blasphemous book or not?

What was the name of his troop commander during his military service?

Is there a difference between a ladies' man and a man of principles?

Has he read the Koran and/or *Capital*?

Does he work in an agronomic institute and teach rural sociology there?

Does he have two or three children from his extraconjugal relationship?

How many times has he been imprisoned and for what reasons?

Is it true that, when questioned about religion, Einstein agreed to subscribe to Islam?

Is *The Prophet* by Khalil Gibran a blasphemous book or not? (Mahfoudh got a secret pleasure out of answering this question, asked twice, once with yes and once with no.)

His activities during the war of independence.

How many times has he attempted to stir up other citizens against the regime in place?

How many times has he traveled abroad?

Did he contact enemies of the state there?

Has he been a spy before and on whose behalf?

His address.

His date of birth.

His name.

The interrogation over, the man with the wood-cutter's build pretends to arrange and then skim the smudged pages. He gets up without interrupting his reading, then leaves the room.

Motionless in his chair, Mahfoudh waits for more than half an hour. He tries to guess the outcome of this masquerade. Ludicrous or deplorable? Perhaps they'll bring him a confession to sign or a deposition he won't even be able to read in this half-light to which his eyes still haven't grown accustomed. Perhaps they'll bring him a prison uniform before taking him to a jail cell. To be sure, he isn't terribly worried but can't explain why. The silence, the dim light, and his immobility make him sleepy. He believes he dozed off when he hears the door open. He turns sideways and sees not the wood-cutter but the two inspectors. They ask him to follow them, and he finds himself in the commissioner's office at last.

This man doesn't immediately react to Mahfoudh's presence, so he stands, thinking that the role of the police, even before that of keeping the order, is first of all to humiliate. A person who stands like this for half an hour or forty-five minutes will have plenty of time to stimulate his bad conscience and let things fester and come to a head; he will have time to search the garbage dump of his past in order to exhume the contemptible acts that the all-powerful authority before him needs to know about in order to pronounce its sentence. A person who stands like this, he tells himself, is already defeated; all they ask of him is that, while rummaging through his miserable life, he establish the proof of his guilt himself.

Finally the commissioner raises his head. Mahfoudh feels like a worm in front of him. He knows that his life has been scrutinized from top to bottom during the "observation period" he has just been through. He knows that, in spite of a specific article in the country's constitution guaranteeing the privacy of correspondence, his mail has been opened and read, his personnel file at school and his bank account have been reviewed, and his phone has been tapped. Once, at school, when he came into the principal's office unannounced, he discovered someone there he didn't know, who he was sure had come from the police and was busy consulting the files of some of his colleagues. The principal had turned pale but recovered right away without, however, introducing the person shuffling through the files.

The commissioner suddenly displays a most affable smile and shows Mahfoudh a seat. "Please, Mr. Lemdjad, do sit down."

Mahfoudh complies.

"I believe you are having difficulties with your passport," the commissioner continues.

"Yes, indeed," says Mahfoudh, "and I am very eager to know what is causing the problem."

"But there isn't any problem," the commissioner declares. "It is merely a bureaucratic oversight we shall correct right away."

"I was convinced there was a snag."

"What made you think there was a snag?"

"I had that notion when I came here a month ago. My previous passport, too, had been difficult to obtain. I believe something here is a little fishy. Surely you are aware that I have just been interrogated."

"I had specifically requested that you be brought to my office straightaway. Your detour was a mistake. You will never know what it's like to work with people whose intelligence is not their primary characteristic."

"Allow me to say that I believe it was neither a mistake nor an oversight. I am still convinced it was more intentional and more serious than that."

"But why? Are you reproaching yourself for something? Do you have a criminal record?"

"Nothing really serious other than a conviction twelve years ago that was subsequently overturned."

"And what was the charge?"

"Breach of national security," Mahfoudh answers very calmly.

"What?!" the commissioner cries out, jumping in his chair and almost swallowing his cigarette.

He is silent for a moment and then asks, "What exactly did you do?"

"I was caught in the last line of a student demonstration, that was all."

"That is of no interest to me. This time you can go down to the magistrate's office and get your passport. It will be ready in two or three days."

And the commissioner rises, thereby inviting Lemdjad to leave.

Even before he gets his passport, Mahfoudh begins to prepare for and plan his trip. He decides to return first to Sidi-Mebrouk, where he has left his paperwork and materials.

He arrives midmorning the next day. As he parks his Volkswagen, he feels unexpectedly emotional. Having worked here enthusiastically and anxiously for days on end, listening to the trees rustle and smelling their fragrance at night, being awakened by the birds at dawn,

Mahfoudh recognizes that, without knowing or even suspecting it, he feels deeply, perhaps inextricably connected to this place. Maybe from now on Sidi-Mebrouk will be part of the landscapes so dear to his heart, together with the old casbah of the capital and the esplanade by the sea with its fountain and its newsstands.

Mahfoudh opens the squeaking door and goes into the large room that saw the birth of his machine. His heart starts pounding as soon as he pushes the door open. The memory of the two spies suddenly comes back to him and, with that, a certain fear. No, the machine, the various materials, as well as the paperwork are all there. Mahfoudh sighs with relief, then goes through the other rooms like a householder who has been absent too long and wants to bathe again in the air of familiar things.

He returns to the main room, picks up a model of the machine, and makes it run. Then he goes over to the documents and stands there for a moment, dazed— they've been handled and aren't in the order in which he left them. Mahfoudh looks around, searching his memory. It is obvious now—many things have been moved and put back more or less where they were. The window lock has been forced. Someone has been here.

Mahfoudh's first feeling is one of deliverance. The intruders could have broken the samples of his machine and destroyed his diagrams. He doesn't know whether he would then have had the courage to start from scratch and reconstruct everything. Since he escaped that disaster, the rest represents no more than a rectifiable obstruction.

Mahfoudh opens the windows wide to let in the outside air, full of spring fragrances and the buzzing of insects. Before putting his things to rights, he decides to take a tour of gratitude, a casual walk through the city with which he feels he has begun an affair that won't end anytime soon.

It is a gorgeous day. The sky is a dazzling blue, dense as a gemstone. A small sun-filled cloud wanders through. The fertile colors of spring are everywhere, clinging to the hedges bordering some homes, to the abundance of insects, to the anarchic and triumphant grasses, and to the trees drowning in foliage.

Mahfoudh heads for the animated center of the little town, where the most important stores are squeezed in with the three cafés—two side by side and the third across the street. Mahfoudh chooses the last one, perhaps because of the promise of its name, the Café of the Future, but most of all because it looks out over the tree-filled square, part of which it uses as a terrace. A rotisserie is working nearby, sending out whiffs of grilled meat.

Mahfoudh sits down on the terrace and orders coffee, whose flavor, as he expected, leaves something to be desired. For a few months now, the only coffee to be found on the market is a "mixed variety" (the packages never indicate the nature of the mix nor its proportions). Alerted to this fact, Mahfoudh doesn't consider the taste of coffee very important. Had he been the least bit preoccupied with the quality of what he's drinking, he would have asked for tea, fruit juice, or lemon soda, products also not entirely beyond suspicion but much less dubious than coffee. What he is after more than anything else is to sit on the terrace, stretch his legs in the sun, and, for a short while, feel like an ordinary citizen at loose ends in a city where he has felt both inspired and persecuted.

He has also come to this particular café in the undeclared hope of a revelation, of some sign or other that would help him understand Sidi-Mebrouk's attitude toward him. Perhaps he will catch a glance or some form of behavior that would guide him to some plot.

Flies and bees are soaring around with a barely perceptible sound of wings, a tiny resonant touch in the multicolored symphony of this sunny day. Occasionally they grow brazen and settle on the table to lick the sticky circles left by glasses of lemon soda or tea.

Once he has finished his coffee, sipping it distractedly and almost without noticing, Mahfoudh stays a good while longer to savor this restorative leisure. What he is hoping, deep down (it is now well past noon), is that he'll see one of the only two people he knows in Sidi-Mebrouk—the custodian of the town hall or the secretary-general. At the same time, however, he knows quite well that the chances are slim—those kinds of people, the second in particular, don't hang around on the streets or in cafés.

He finally gets up and heads for Rabah Talbi's house, where he piles everything he might need for his trip to Heidelberg into the Volkswagen bug.

PART TWO

From the sea, the city looks like stacks of over-lapping cubes, a complex checkerboard of terraces. It gives the impression of a gigantic beehive, compact and closed, hiding a multitude of mysteries. It is a vista sought after by landscape hunters—painters, photog-raphers, film directors—in their rush to freeze and eternalize it before proximity destroys the beauty that distance has sculpted. Little rectangles cut out by the snapping of cameras. Scenery sold as postcards. Those who don't know the old city and see it only from afar could actually dream of it as a secret network of alley-ways, miniature palaces, cool atria, and places that dis-pense miracles, causing one to shiver. The fertile and freethinking imagination can flit through places meant for harrowing but never fatal adventures in which money, courage, terror, fidelity or betrayal, and love all come together in the end.

While he follows the seagulls' elliptical paths, Mah-foudh, too, is dreaming, but of something else. Once again he realizes how lackluster the capital city is—a scattering of districts or rather communities, wedged between the sea and the side of a mountain. Some quarters still smell of sweating horses and of passing herds of goats. To this very day, roosters awaken you. There is nothing here of other world capitals and their interplay of billboards and neon lights, their iridescence, their stratified urban texture that tell the long story of streetlights, electricity, tunnels, squares, fountains, spectacles, and cars. Here stone, hay, and animals live in close proximity; you only need to scratch the surface to see and inhale them. The city's only treasure is its light, which sizzles like quicklime. It has known daring periods that made its sails billow and propelled it toward unknown places rich in enticements and dangers. But those periods do not last forever. The city is a lazy homebody, turning its back on the sea again, breaking every connection with the open water, and finding refuge among its rocks.

Mahfoudh is looking at the seagulls, steadily growing in number. The light splinters off into sequins, dancing to an imperceptible rhythm. The scoured sky glistens like blue enamel. Below, the sea spreads its new-metal glow. The colors here are tolerable only for tried-and-true eyes.

The trip to Heidelberg was intensely gratifying. Mahfoudh had time to visit the castle, Wittelsbach, the old university, and the tiny laboratory where Robert Bun-

sen perfected his gas burner. But he is happy to be back
in this city of limestone and granite. He loves it like a
sanctuary, like the bosom of a caring family. For him it
is the cozy shelter of childhood, the domain of dreams,
effort, and painful and true passions all at the same
time. He wouldn't be able to live away from this city for
long. He returns today as the prodigal son, a conqueror,
with that pretty, unanticipated trophy. No, he really had
not expected to receive a prize at the prestigious Heidelberg Inventors' Fair. This makes his pleasure all the
greater. He cannot wait to be back on land so that his
compatriots can hear all about his victory.

Now the rocky shore is coming closer, revealing its
protrusions—houses, roads, ramparts, everything is
seen through the screen of a fine mist, a dancing veil of
water. The ship will soon enter the bay's gigantic arc.

When the boat slowly approaches the pier, while the
seagulls serenade him, Mahfoudh begins to feel a name-
less anxiety. Every time he comes back from traveling
and has to deal with customs, he has the same feeling.
Leaning on the ship's rail, he watches the city pulsate in
the harsh light. He is impatient to be moving around in
its heat and noise, to sit on the terrace of one of its cafés.
But first he must brave the line in front of the passport
window and then the customs officers themselves. He
tries not to think about that moment. He'll close his

128 TAHAR DJAOUT

eyes for a long time, and, when he opens them, he'll be on the other side, in the fresh air, in the city, without barriers or controls.

Not having been very alert, Mahfoudh finds himself almost at the end of one of the two disorderly lines stretching ever farther as more travelers disembark—especially since both booths are empty. One of them has not yet opened, and the other was abandoned by its agent after ten minutes. The immense and badly ventilated hall is like an oven.

The travelers are nervous, impatient, and plagued with worry. It is as if they were going to be cross-examined, not merely completing a formality. All of them are therefore ready for a fight, eager to be done with an interrogation you never come out of unscathed, and to move on to count their losses and rejoice over what was saved. There is a lot of pushing and shoving, and altercations erupt at regular intervals. The most brazen of the passengers move ahead of the line in a roundabout way, sliding up ten, sometimes fifteen places. It's hard to believe that these individuals, light-years away from civility and courtesy, are the same as those who were exchanging pleasantries on the ship's bridge just a few minutes before; the same as those who will insist on buying you a cup of coffee if they run into you in town tomorrow.

Chaos ensues when the customs officers return to

their booths. Both lines shudder, break apart, and come together again, while most of the passengers jockey for a spot, or at least try not to lose the one they have, by sticking very close to the person in front of them. It is as if a frenzied wave were throwing them one against the other.

A new issue quickly revives the spirits of those waiting: a piece of information goes from mouth to ear along the lines—one of the agents is stricter than the other, spends more time checking papers, is a real nitpicker. Many of the anxious travelers now try to change lines. Then another bit of news makes the rounds: new rules have been established. Regarding what exactly? Nobody has any details.

These alarming shreds of information have added to the crowd's uneasiness, increasing the pushing and shoving, and provoking questions and conversations.

Mahfoudh would give anything to see the water. It would make his wait more bearable. But this hot place with all its squashing has not a single window on the water. Still, Mahfoudh tries to imagine the sea. Rippled by an easygoing breeze, its surface covered with claw-edged wavelets as far as the eye can see. He is overworking his imagination. It's the same when he suffers from insomnia and tries to focus his attention on a specific landscape until sleep overtakes him.

Suddenly, what everyone expected happens. The long-smoldering crisis explodes. Shrill screaming rises from the front of one of the lines. A woman's voice erupts in accusations. This spreads enormous comfort among the people waiting. It is as if an abscess has burst. Tongues are loosened, bonds are forged, and friendships begin to form. They were a sweating, trampling line; now they are becoming human beings again, endowed with words, manners, judgment, and a sharp sense of values. The woman who just recovered her voice and her indignation made this her gift to all of them. She destroyed the omnipotence of the impregnable booth, indifferent to the heat and the resentment that torment the bodies inside, cunningly leveling them. Once the crowd's tongue has been unleashed, it bypasses criticism, giving shape to its words, ideas, and questions. The people wonder what exactly is happening inside the glass booth. Those close enough to see impart the information to the others. It arrives magnified, picking up details and commentary as it progresses down the line. Mahfoudh is among the privileged who are able to get some details from the very source of the squabble—only three people separate him from the glass booth, and he was able to see and hear the dispute. It concerns a problem of names: the name of the screaming woman is the same as that of a wanted person.

When Mahfoudh reaches the glass booth he can go right through. The agent, no doubt rattled by his skirmish with the lady, has lost both his authority and his inflexibility.

Mahfoudh is glad to be back in fresh air. The first phase of his dealings with the harbor authorities is over. He wonders whether the conditions won't be more trying when he comes back in a few days to retrieve his machine, shipped by the organizing committee of the Heidelberg Fair. But he decides not to think about it; he prefers to limit his horizon to the next two or three days, during which he can rest up from the excitement of his trip and share the happy surprise of his award with his friends.

The container with his material arrives five days later. Mahfoudh presents himself at the harbor, armed with the telegram from Heidelberg. The first person he approaches informs him that form E68 has to be submitted before anything can be claimed.

"What form is that?"

"It's a form provided by a forwarding agent. There's one over there. He can explain it to you."

Mahfoudh follows the signs to the other agent.

"Form E68? That will be forty thousand centimes. I need your ticket and a photocopy of the document describing your goods."

"The container didn't travel with me. It was sent to me."

"In that case, the second document will be enough."

There is no copy machine at the harbor, so Mahfoudh has to go back into town. When he returns, the agent in question is about to close up, but he fills out form E68 anyway because Mahfoudh must have aroused his sympathy.

It isn't noon yet, and Mahfoudh hurries to a row of offices, two of which are still open. He enters the nearest one and offers the form to a man who, without even asking what he wants, spitefully taunts him: "I see we have to go without lunch today in order to satisfy the gentleman's wishes."

"What should I do with this form, then?"

"Come back at two o'clock, I suppose. But if you have a better solution, feel free to suggest it."

Once again, Mahfoudh goes back into town. He has a quick lunch in a mediocre restaurant, but consumes half a liter of wine to calm his nerves a little and compose himself in order to face the rest of the affair.

It is one-thirty when he starts back to the harbor. He wanders around a little on the way, planning to arrive just as the offices reopen. Positioned right in the center of the sky, the sun seems abandoned there, and the heat is as heavy as a tombstone.

Mahfoudh arrives at the harbor at ten after two, but the offices take another good fifteen minutes to open. This time Mahfoudh manages to get his form E68 stamped and is cleared to enter an open hall adjoining an immense platform where containers, cars, and various crates are visible. A wire fence with a gate separates the hall from the platform. There to reclaim a car or other goods, many people are waiting resignedly for the gate between them and their possessions to open. From time to time they vent a stream of reflections and commentary, bitter but never blaming, and the overall atmosphere is one of submission.

When the gate doesn't seem to be opening anytime soon, Mahfoudh turns to the well-dressed person next to him and expresses some highly impolite thoughts regarding the harbor department. But the man first averts his face and then actually walks away from Mahfoudh, as if afraid to compromise himself and complicate a situation that is already far from brilliant. He looks determined to submit to another two, three, or four hours in the sweltering sun provided they let him take his car and go home, where he'll quickly forget the whole experience.

Suddenly all eyes are turning to the same point—the harbor inspector is coming. His tall build and his soldier's stride are impressive. When he is a few yards away from the human herd, which has clustered close to the gate in the hope it will finally swing back, he stops, glances at the riffraff, and shouts in an authoritarian voice full of reproach: "What's keeping you from picking your stuff up? You're not planning on spending the whole year cluttering up the harbor, are you?"

Most of them quite simply lower their heads or look

in another direction. But one person, braver than the rest, takes the initiative and explains: "Picking up is all we want to do, but the gate is closed."

"Well then, we'll get them to unlock it for you," the inspector answers with the same military efficiency.

Making a bullhorn out of his hands, he yells at a young customs officer on the other side of the platform guarding a barred passage: "Open this gate for us!"

"I don't have the key, El Hadj does," the other man calls from afar.

"Try anyway, just make an effort."

Dumbfounded, the crowd then sees the young man climb up a barrier, throw his leg over it, and, like a tightrope walker, hang there on a railing twenty yards above the street where cars are rushing by. Having made it to the gate that seals off the platform from his side, he grabs it, then hoists himself up, his legs dangling in the air. On the other side and with bated breath, the people are watching the movements and then the wriggling of the young agent, finally understanding that he is trying to land on the esplanade in order to open the gate from the inside. He keeps pushing and wriggling, clinging to the gate's grillwork like a spider to its web. Then, weary, he gives up his Sisyphean effort, remains motionless for a moment as if to gather his strength, and descends slowly to put his feet on the railing. He straddles the barrier and is back where he began. His agitation, no doubt, was enormous, like that of his audience, which didn't utter a word the whole time he was suspended between sky and street.

For a few seconds the young agent is silent (perhaps he's speaking softly, but on the other side nobody hears anything), then with his face glued to the gate he blurts out angrily: "I think you want me dead, General. Just wait for El Hadj, the old poke, or else get lost."

The inspector, afraid to lose face for having been so disrespectfully told off, turns to the waiting group: "He only wanted to help us," he explains. "It's not his job to open the gate. He has to guard the driveway, nothing else."

At that moment old El Hadj arrives, an hour and a half late. He walks with a limp, jingling a bunch of keys in his hand. As he goes to the gate the people move aside to let him through, the way one moves aside for safety when a dog with a bad reputation passes by on a leash. It would seem that no one wants anything to do with him. No one, not even the inspector, dares criticize him.

The gate opens at last. People wait for El Hadj to leave, then rush to the platform, turn ignition keys or grab their gear, and start to move through inspection as fast as possible. The three lanes at the end of which the customs agents stand are soon chock-full of cars and bundles. Mahfoudh, case in hand, finds himself in the center corridor. The lines are moving very slowly. One agent has made a driver unload his entire van, open every package and suitcase, and rip open the bundles; then he makes the poor devil close everything up again, repack, and reload while he goes to have a chat with a colleague or get a cup of coffee at the snack bar. He seems to know exactly how much time is needed to redo everything he has undone, for he reappears at the very moment the next passenger begins to put down his baggage for inspection.

Mahfoudh observes also that some agents—notably a little old man with a cap too big for his head who, in view of his age, should have been retired (unless he's a lot younger than he looks)—are unabashedly swiping apples, bananas, chocolate bars, cigarettes, and even underwear from the bags of passengers who, distraught to watch their possessions disappear this way, don't know where to turn. One passenger "chosen" by an agent's greed has a most unexpected reaction—he actually smiles, as if the possessive familiarity with which the agent honors him creates fellowship between them. Once inspected, the passenger moves his car or baggage aside so that the next in line can move up. He goes into a booth where he must get a paper and then pay a fee before coming back to receive an exit slip. Mahfoudh notices that before heading for the booth, someone who has just been fleeced may pull one of the authorities into a corner (a customs agent, one of the agents in the booth, sometimes even the inspector himself) and slip something into his hand or pocket. Money, of course— currency exchangeable in the country from which he came. He wonders what they are paying off with this bribe. The mistreatment they've just suffered, or the fear of being subjected to further and subtler abuses later on?

At last Mahfoudh reaches the customs agent.

"That's all you have?" he exclaims reproachfully.

"Yes," Mahfoudh responds.

The agent snorts. Nobody would come up with the idea of going to a country of affluence, comfort, ready goods, to a country where money is meant to be spent, and come back with nothing but a plain box.

"Open it," he says abruptly.

"We'll need pliers. Do I really have to open it? I have a document here that describes the contents. It's a small machine I invented."

The agent's doubts are beginning to turn into confidence. He's dealing with a special case here! He is so pleased with his good fortune that he allows himself a joke: "If I understand it correctly, you invent machines far away from home and then have them sent to you."

"No, no, I invented it here."

"So you sent it abroad for approval! Let's have a look at this precious machine."

He comes back with pliers and a hammer, cuts the metal wire, and pulls out the small nails.

"What is all that?" he asks as he contemplates the pretty assemblage of wooden pieces.

"It's a loom."

"Aha! I thought it was a puppet with broken joints. You see how disappointed I am . . ."

"But why?"

"Because I was expecting a real machine—a miniature spacecraft, a household robot, or a computer. All you've invented is an old woman's tool. You don't live here? You don't know that our country is committed to walking the path of modernism? Why don't you go out into the street someday instead of staying cloistered in your house and take a look at the cable cars, the electronic games and news. Perhaps that'll give you ideas for other inventions."

Mahfoudh doesn't know how to respond to this avalanche of criticism. Enormous disappointment, even a kind of contempt shows on the face of the other man.

"Better swaddle your baby again," he says as he turns his back on him and goes off to describe his frustration at the snack bar, no doubt.

Mahfoudh fits the machine back into its packing as best he can. He stashes it in a corner and heads for the booth to obtain the form that will let him make the payment. When he enters, the agent is just leaving without a glance in his direction, as if there were no one else in the booth. Fifteen minutes later he returns, riffles through his files, and announces he has no forms left. Since Mahfoudh doesn't seem to understand what attitude to take in this situation, the agent asks him to leave while he looks for more forms.

Once outside the booth, Mahfoudh begins to wonder whether he is being subjected to the additional bullying because he failed to fulfill some other obligation. Suddenly, it hits him—he should have slipped him some money before entering the booth, one of the essential elements of this part of the battle. Obviously, he must let it go now, abruptly drained of all impatience and all rebellion; still, he is curious to find out how far his infringement of this "rule" will take him.

Not until his second attempt does the agent let him enter the booth at last. Silently and carelessly, with the motions of an outraged lord, he stamps the file and throws it at Mahfoudh. But Mahfoudh doesn't need to ask for directions; he knows where to go next.

Without losing any time he heads for the accounts department. It is very near, but on that side its door is closed. To enter, one must walk along an interminable barricade, reenter the administrative block, and go along a series of hallways. Finally, he arrives at the office in question. He knocks, opens the door, and sees a bald, wretched-looking old gentleman with glasses, collapsed in his chair like Job on top of his dunghill.

The employee gives Mahfoudh a look of bafflement

and disdain, a look filled with aggression and blame, as if the person standing before him were responsible for his advanced age, his ugliness, his decline—in short, for the sum total of his miseries.

"I'm here to pay," Mahfoudh says, holding out the paper.

The old man grabs the form, scribbles a few words, then hands Mahfoudh a bill. He takes out his check-book, tears out a check, and starts to complete it. Only then does the old man open his mouth.

"What are you doing?"

"I'm writing a check."

"To whom if I may ask?"

"To pay the amount you've just shown me."

The old man gives him a long, curious look, at once dumbfounded and offended, as if Mahfoudh had just pronounced some inexcusable words of abuse. His face is furrowed by a succession of tics, revealing God knows what emotion. Something like a smile begins to show, then vanishes. And what finally comes out of the man's mouth, as he hides behind his glasses, is a tremulous and whimpering voice: "And of course the gentleman thinks I'm going to accept his check?"

Since Mahfoudh doesn't seem to understand, the old man barks, outraged, "How do I know your check is good? Why don't you pay cash like everyone else?"

Forcing himself to stay calm, Mahfoudh explains that

he doesn't wander around with a safe in his arms, that he didn't even know he would have to pay to retrieve his possessions, that he did have cash with him this morning but that form E68 and lunch in town had cleaned him out.

The sly little man reacts in a most surprising way. Perhaps he is persuaded of Mahfoudh's good faith, disarmed by his naïveté. In any event, he goes so far as to smile behind his mustache and glasses, a solid smile that ripples his bald head. He holds out his hand for the check.

Mahfoudh looks at his watch. He is haunted by the fear of arriving too late at the booth where he must get his exit slip and having to return the next day. He runs out of the old man's office, veering sharply down the hallways. The booth is still open. He barrels in, receipt in hand. This time the agent, surely in a hurry to leave, hands him his exit slip right away.

Clutching the precious trophy, Mahfoudh leaves. He sighs with relief—finally he can go home; the only thing left to do is to show his slip to the police at the exit, a simple formality involving no bargaining or intimidation. He looks at the sea, whose presence he had forgotten from the minute he was heading for the first agent's window. He inhales deeply.

When he is about to put the exit slip in his pocket he notices with horror that it's not in his name. For a few moments he stands unsettled. Then he dashes across the inspection area and over the esplanade leading toward the exit, calling out the name on his slip. Fortunately, the person to whom it belongs is still there, busily stowing his load in his van before driving off. He shows the slip he has—it has Mahfoudh's name on it. A simple exchange is all that is required.

Dangling the container from his hand, Mahfoudh at last leaves the harbor compound. It is ten after six. He can already see his red Volkswagen waiting for him like a beacon in the parking lot, just two hundred yards away.

The cultural page and the sports page are the only ones Mahfoudh looks at (and possibly reads) in the *Incorruptible Militant*. So it is Samia, a more eclectic and willing reader, who discovers the small item between the column devoted to parliamentary life and an article on reforestation. They are in the living room. They're talking about this and that (the windows are closed because of the noise coming in from a construction site) while waiting to have lunch.

Suddenly, Samia, who's skimming through the paper without really reading it, cries out, "Well, look at this!"

Mahfoudh, his curiosity aroused, comes over immediately. Then he reads the following:

National Inventor Receives Prize at Heidelberg Fair

Thanks to the efforts and know-how of its children, our country is gradually occupying an enviable place in the concert of nations. Most recently, there were the crushing World Cup victories in which every patriotic citizen trembled at our beautiful performance, as well as at our superiority on the

Continent this year, recognized by two trophies: the
Cup and the Championship of Nations. Today, our
victory lies in another domain, equally as presti-
gious as that of the artificial turf: the field of tech-
nology. Indeed, Mr. Mahfoudh Lemdjad, a local
teacher just 34 years old, caused a sensation at the
Inventors' Fair in Heidelberg, where he received an
award. His machine, an updated loom, symbolizes
our nation's double demand, the challenge directed
both at the past and at the future: shouldering
modernity while keeping our roots intact. This new
trophy, added to those that already adorn our col-
lective memory, honors our country and at the
same time opens the way for other unrecognized
geniuses, other creative imaginations that, no
doubt, will not be long in coming forth.

Mahfoudh continues on to the next article, as if it
were on the same subject:

Following the demonstrations organized by small
groups of students, the National Secretariat of the
General Workers Union held a meeting on Tues-
day. It analyzed the present political situation,
which is marked by a mood of disturbance due to
certain biased elements working for the interests of
imperialists, reactionaries, and their followers, and
proclaiming slogans that run counter to the for-

ward movement and continuation of the Revolution. After the bitter blow the popular masses of the Revolution dealt the reactionaries, the latter have not ceased redoubling their tactics and challenging the masses, who have brought home so many victories and effected important gains in industry, agriculture, and culture.

Reappearing on the scene of today's events with new methods, the reactionaries this time have chosen the popular national legacy as a shield, a principle clearly stated in the National Charter for whose protection and preservation the masses labor. Indeed, these desperate attempts, inscribed in the framework of a broad plan developed by the reactionaries, aim at attacking the country's sovereignty, national unity, the Revolution, and the people's gains. Faced with this situation, the National Secretariat of the General Workers Union, convinced of the attachment of the masses to the National Charter, believes in the political will of the direction that resulted from the Party's Fourth Congress, to work for realizing the Revolution's objectives, and is aware of the strong positions taken by our workers at crucial moments and under the difficult conditions the country faces. The National Secretariat denounces the enemies of the Revolution wherever they may be and whatever veil they

may hide behind to execute their vile maneuvers.
Wholly convinced it is expressing the deep-seated
aspirations of the masses, it is renewing its abso-
lute support for the President of the Republic, the
Secretary-General of the Party, with the defense
and continuation of the Revolution, as well as the
consolidation of its gains, in mind. It calls upon
the workers, who are the soldiers of the Revolution,
to pursue the task relentlessly in order to be the
bulwark against which any imperialist and re-
actionary assault will be crushed.

Not until he has read almost the entire article, which is of no concern to him, does Mahfoudh begin to ask himself some questions: Who could have written the article about him? Where did the information come from? It must be the national press agency, which has an office in Germany, that gave out the news. Some journalist, running out of ideas and not having written anything for weeks, cleaned up and embellished the press release to combine the country, soccer, and science in the same resounding tribute.

Mahfoudh is very pleased with this official recognition by the media, a revenge on the petty bureaucracy incapable of making the distinction of what is and what is not truly great. He pictures all those who bullied and humiliated him—policemen, bureaucrats, secretaries-

general of various sorts, commissioners, custodians—
reading this news and biting their fingernails for having
acted with such lack of insight. He has no doubt that
the whole fine group of them has read the article in the
Incorruptible Militant. He thinks of the far smaller number who tried to help him and tells himself that this
tribute in a way reflects on them, too. He wonders how
to digest this, discuss it with Samia, and relish the unexpected recognition in peace.

Below, the street vibrates with all sorts of sounds.
For several days, workmen have been doing their utmost to give the neighborhood a new face. An incessant
racket dominates. When the jackhammers fall silent,
other less deafening but equally intolerable noises start
up—concrete mixers, elevators, badly oiled cables, each
with its own musical sound. The question is whether all
these aggressive machines, all these bandages and super-
ficial repairs, will manage to safeguard this sick artery of
the city. It is difficult to breathe easily in this pudgy, out-
of-breath town, burdened by numerous open sores and
at every moment threatened with a coronary.

The place where those making Sidi-Mebrouk's history congregate is no more than a kind of shed in what serves as a parking lot for the town hall. There is the fourth-term mayor himself, the secretary-general, the city planner, and the custodian. The only one missing is the postmaster, who left that morning to straighten out a problem at the magistrate's offices and who should have been back long ago.

They didn't want to meet in an office where an intruder or a superior, arriving unexpectedly from the district office, the magistrate's office, or the Party's headquarters, could take them by surprise and start asking prying questions.

They therefore chose to hold their secret meeting in the middle of the day. They won't have lunch today, but the sacrifice is well worth it. The situation is complex, delicate, and serious, and must be sorted out as quickly as possibly. They have read the news and spent three days quaking in their boots, waiting for the reaction of the higher authorities. Nothing having happened yet, they decide to take the initiative.

The mayor briefly summarizes a few facts just for form so as not to pose too abruptly the question that is troubling all of them: "When they ask us for explanations, how will we justify our rather unseemly behavior toward an inventor who has just been praised in the newspapers?"

He drops his customary arrogance to solicit the judgment, intelligence, and tactical sense of his subordinates (whom he usually treats with the haughtiness of a primate faced with single-cell creatures). His collaborators remain silent, fearful of stepping onto a minefield. Nobody dares take it upon himself to break the silence, to suggest a strategy whose consequences will be serious, a strategy that could just as easily salvage and exonerate the municipal government as bring about its downfall.

At that moment of great bewilderment the door of the shed is gently pushed open and the postmaster, looking ashen, stands on the threshold. He is terrified of the mayor. He comes forward, shaking as if he were going to be shot, and sputters a tremulous greeting. But no one looks at him nor responds to his civilities. Silence reigns. Then Skander Brik, who can't be bothered with fussy rhetoric and intellectual quibbling, speaks up to suggest an approach. "What we need," he says, "is a scapegoat to pull us out of this predicament."

Such cynical and practical candor leaves the others delighted and relieved, but also cautious. They wait for someone else to back Skander's thought, which is as obvious as it is bold. Again silence. Now that an opening has been made, everyone waits for the mayor's opinion. He knows it, too, and decides to speak.

"It is the voice of wisdom expressing itself through the mouth of our custodian. And all of you know that wisdom sometimes is ruthless. It is not concerned with the means, but interested only in great goals. As some proverb or other states, or perhaps it is simply my own logic, when there is gangrene in a hand one shouldn't hesitate to cut it off in order to protect the health of the rest of the body. I shall therefore let you think this over, but I don't doubt for one moment that your decision has already been made with the clarity, cohesion, and resolve that characterize us in all unequivocal circumstances."

It is very hot in the shed, but the atmosphere is more relaxed now that the mayor has spoken. Two men clear their throats and some whispering follows. The hunt for the gangrenous hand is on. Voices are preparing to be heard and inscribed into the history of Sidi-Mebrouk.

Finally the secretary-general makes up his mind, for he knows that neither of the two others, having remained silent, will dare take the floor before he does. He is going to start his presentation with the sacred religious formula ("In the name of the merciful and compassionate God . . .") but changes his mind, for he is afraid the mayor, who spoke up without any formula or invocation, will take it as implied criticism.

"As we knew he would," he says instead, "the mayor has spoken once again with the efficiency and seriousness the situation requires. Yes, we are facing a task of considerable importance: protecting the health of our administration, our city, and our country. And I therefore add my humble voice to that of our mayor—we must not have pity on afflicted limbs that may contaminate the entire body."

Now it is the city planner's turn to enter the debate. He has no great demagogic experience and goes ahead without any particular subtlety: "If I've understood it correctly, we must find a convenient culprit who won't be able to besmirch us. We certainly should find him if we want to get out while the going is good."

It is the postmaster's turn to express his point of view or rather to approve and reinforce the one expressed by the others. But he is so disconcerted by his lateness and so terrified of the mayor that he can't bring himself to open his mouth. The formality of his opinion doesn't seem to carry any great weight, and it is Skander who starts up again. "To be honest, I have already thought of the person who can put us in the clear."

All eyes are on him, questioning and hopeful. He

allows a few seconds to go by, then continues: "I'm thinking of Menouar Ziada."

The mayor immediately responds. "Does he fit the necessary profile? Is there any evidence against him?"

"Of course," Skander replies. "Otherwise I wouldn't have picked him."

The others, all of whom know Menouar, cannot help but be surprised. They were expecting a more obvious choice, a notorious counterrevolutionary, an avowed liberal, someone who voted no in the elections (the envelopes are almost transparent, and it is easy to see the color of the ballots inside them), an unorthodox rich man who had the misfortune of gaining wealth through his own schemes and not, like honest people, by dipping into the State's coffers. Menouar seems to be a rather bloodless figure to them, an ineffectual prey that is not much of a catch. A feeling of uneasiness sets in.

Then the city planner ventures to ask, "What can we accuse him of?"

"Many things, believe me," Skander asserts.

"Then we must establish the grievances in order to make the charges," the postmaster finally suggests in a whimpering voice.

He begins to sweat copiously, not so much from the heat in the shed as from the superhuman effort he has just made to drive the mountain of words from his head to his mouth.

Skander, who could have disregarded him, pushes his generosity and courtesy to the extreme and provides him with an explanation. "What we must have," he stipulates, "is someone who won't put up any resistance, not by himself nor by having others intervene, someone who won't oppose our reasoning with his own, who might well even disappear before we're asked to argue and show proof."

"However, let's not forget that Menouar is a veteran," the city planner objects.

"Precisely," Skander continues. "That is not a shining episode of his life, and I happen to know some very unflattering details about it. Menouar was almost executed as a traitor by our own people. I'm sure there are other things from that period he wouldn't like us to talk about."

"But what has that got to do with the present issue?" the secretary-general inquires.

"Wasn't he the first one aware of Mahfoudh Lemdjad's presence in our town? Instead of alerting us, he kept the secret to himself. From there to his being responsible for the troubles the inventor encountered is not a big step to take."

They all remain silent in the face of Skander's diabolical reasoning. Are they to back him up or, on the contrary, be appalled? Their feelings are of no importance. All they know is that they're prisoners of the ruthless custodian's recommendation, that they must submit to his logic and follow it to the bitter end without the possibility of turning around or even of stopping to ask themselves any questions.

Skander now acts like the criminal who is ready to confess, pushing aside the last vestiges of caution and decency, demeaning himself in order to be let off the hook. He speaks as if in a trance, not looking at anyone in particular, not even at the mayor.

"I chose Menouar not only because he won't put up any resistance but also because he is a rather useless member of our society. He hasn't even produced any children to defend him or, at the very least, mourn him. We all agree on one point: the objective of all our actions must be the health of our society. The loss of Menouar will be a pruning, not an amputation; it is a loss that will affect no one. He will disappear like a letter in the mail. I actually believe everyone will benefit from it."

The mayor looks at his watch. They have another twenty minutes left to refine the process, to set a strategy in motion that will wash the town hall of its sins and bring honor to the national spirit. The culprit has been found—all that remains is to make his crime known. At the same time, a committee has to prepare the celebration at which the city, chosen by Mahfoudh Lemdjad to join him in posterity, will officially bestow its gratitude upon him.

Having set the practical terms and appointed those who are to implement them, the men making Sidi-Mebrouk's history leave the shed one by one, at intervals of three or four minutes. They look around carefully before making a run for it, then scurry off to the administrative building as fast as they can. The mayor is the last to leave, hugging the walls at first, then trying to look relaxed as he heads back to his office.

This time Skander Brik doesn't even pretend to put on his scar-smile. He looks serious and solemn. He catches Menouar Ziada early in the morning when he leaves his house, as if he'd been waiting for him for hours with the patience of a spider. He comes straight up to him but doesn't speak right away. Not a word is exchanged between them, not even a greeting. They walk together for a little while and then Skander finally says, "I have some very serious things to tell you."

Menouar stops in his tracks but doesn't look at his escort.

"Not here," Skander says. "We could go to my place or to some quiet spot at the edge of the village. But when all is said and done I'd prefer my place. It is the only location where we won't run the risk of being seen or overheard by the indiscreet."

Menouar starts walking, but behind Skander now, no longer by his side.

Skander's house is a small villa surrounded by a wall with shards of glass on top. It used to belong to a family of rich colonizers who owned vast agricultural holdings

in the region. When independence came, Skander took
it over, Chinese submachine gun in hand. Other people
coveted the place—military officers who proposed other
homes to him in exchange—but he rejected every offer
and tenaciously defended his spoils. What appealed to
him above all about the villa was the garden with its
three fruit trees and profusion of flowers. The three trees
(lemon, medlar, and fig) are still there, but the flowers
quickly disappeared to make room for lettuce, onions,
and tomatoes, a miraculously acclimated pepper bush,
and a few bean plants. A ditch cuts through the vegetable garden, its stagnant greenish water discharging a
nauseating odor. This doesn't seem to bother the three
chickens and one guinea fowl that greedily drink there.
The villa's facade, flaking and crumbling in some places,
has been crudely replastered. It was once coated with
what must have been beige paint, but hasn't been re-
done in at least thirty years.

When they enter the house, Menouar hears no
sounds, no voices. Perhaps the setting has been prepared. Perhaps the house is empty so that no one will
overhear the secret. Menouar also realizes that it's his
first time in this house, which really is not normal for
two inhabitants of the same small town who are practically neighbors and, moreover, participated in the same
war. They must have rubbed shoulders frequently to
confront and reduce the staggering demands of the new

society, of the impudent youth who no longer have the same dogmas and causes they had.

Skander's voice pulls him out of his daydreams. In fact, the house is not empty, for the master is calling out to someone invisible: "Woman, make us some coffee."

The two sit down side by side as if embarrassed to be facing each other. Skander speaks: "The State is like God. Both demand our respect and our submission. Moreover, the designs of both are inscrutable and just."

Menouar, silent and uneasy, waits impatiently for the rest. He knows that the best way to figure out what people have against him is to remain silent, not to disturb Skander's train of thought with his comments or questions. The latter begins his story.

"The Mahfoudh Lemdjad affair has taken some unexpected turns. You are going to have to atone for the obstacles you created for him and the suspicions you raised, my good friend."

"But I did nothing of the sort. I didn't cause him any trouble. I've never even seen him."

"That's some weird version that, I'm afraid, only you believe."

Skander's wife comes in with two cups of coffee on a tray. Menouar's heart is racing, his throat is dry, and his mind muddled. He understands that he is in an extremely dangerous position. It is as if he were facing a wild animal and has to react quickly before the claws sink into his chest and throat. But neither his mind nor his mouth manages to find a way out.

After two sips of coffee, Skander continues: "What you're saying is astounding. Everyone high up is talking about this business. Even if the papers haven't gotten hold of it yet, it won't be long before they do if we aren't careful. As far as the mayor and the town hall's secretary-general are concerned, and the leader of the Party and above all Commander Si Abdenour Demik, to whom we owe everything, agree, you are the one responsible for the problems Mahfoudh Lemdjad encountered."

"That is a most regrettable misunderstanding. I will have to explain everything to them."

"They won't need any explanations. They've already made their decision, and the best thing for you to do at this point, for your own and their best interests, is to submit to it."

"A great injustice is about to be done. Who will benefit by an injustice?"

"They know all about it. And, believe me, their decision was not made lightly nor with any joy in their hearts."

"They want me to sacrifice myself?"

"Such is our fate. Every time the country's interest calls us, we must know how to say 'present.' We're lucky we're dealing with courageous men. They steered us in the right direction during our glorious war, and they lead us now."

Menouar can't begin to comprehend the calamity befalling him. In a shaking voice he says, "Do you realize what they're asking of me? What if I won't go along?"

"I'll be frank with you. They'll dig up the war period, some very unfortunate episodes will be brought out, and they'll invent a few more—"

"They'll invent a few more?"

"Yes. Your name will be reviled forever. All the advantages you now enjoy will be taken away from you, your possessions confiscated. You'll live in disgrace."

Skander is silent, looks sideways at his guest, and notices he hasn't touched his coffee. A heavy silence falls between them. Menouar is as gaunt as the twig of an ash tree. Everything about him—head, limbs, bony fingers, puny skeleton—evokes the image of an insect. His whole body starts to tremble as if a sudden fever has hit him. He utters barely audible noises as he clears his throat, and Skander thinks for a moment that he is crying. Finally he pulls himself together and asks the fateful question, the one he's been afraid to ask since the beginning of the interview and which, as long as it remains unasked, keeps him safe from the inevitable, or so it seems to him.

"What do they want me to do?" he utters.

Timidly he looks at Skander and for the first time notices that his staring eyes, piercing and at the same time devoid of any expression, look like those of a vulture. The two hard, black pupils could jump out of the whites of his eyes and kill him like bullets at point-blank range.

Skander takes his time before answering. "They want you to disappear," he finally says, very coldly. "Your suicide will be presented as a gesture of remorse, as an act of profound rationality, the high-priced redemption of an unfortunate mistake committed at the expense of a great inventor. Your name, like that of our town, will be linked with this invention instead of being dragged through the mud."

Skander perseveres like a hunting dog that has smelled blood. The last words, in their harshness, have been meticulously prepared to break down the last protective barrier in the victim, any vague desire to resist or even to protest. The blow seems to have hit home—Menouar sits there, still trembling, haggard, stupefied, suddenly beset by aphasia, mouthing a broth of sounds, words or embryonic ideas that cannot find their shape. His universe is shattered. He doesn't even know where he is. Will he get up and leave? Will he lie down right here and wait for the noose or the knife to bring deliverance? Is the man beside him, sipping his coffee, an angel or a demon? The agent of his destruction or the last salvation he should desperately hang on to? He is overwhelmed with self-pity. He sees his life as a chain of failures and afflictions and wonders whether such a life has really been worth living, whether the solution proposed to him here is, in fact, not the ideal out he should have taken a long time ago in order, once and for all, to shorten this pain they call living.

He thinks of his village, of his father, who died too young and whose features he doesn't even remember, of his sterile man's loneliness. He also and unexpectedly thinks of Moh Saïd, the simpleton, slaughtered like an ordinary sheep, and then he thinks of an episode of his life in the resistance.

His group had just stormed a truck of the army of the occupation, and, after a deadly clash, they had taken one prisoner—a young man with a delicate body, terrified and expecting God knows what tortures. The resistance fighters started back to their hideout with the prisoner in the middle of the line. When they reached their destination, Aliouate, a man who was slightly deranged because he had witnessed the execution of his father and brother by occupying soldiers in his village, rushed toward the prisoner to kill him with his knife. His comrades intervened. He tried two or three more times, then finally calmed down after his buddies took him aside and had a long talk with him. Everyone thought he had given up on his plan. But during the night he rose stealthily and, eluding the sentinels' vigilance, cut the captive's throat (during the young soldier's sleep, no doubt, for there never were any cries).

Menouar closes his eyes and an enormous weight gently begins to melt inside him. His tears are flowing copiously, liberated, serene. It's as if he has delved deep inside himself and reached the delicate and sensitive child, the child whom dishonor and death cannot touch, who can weep unashamedly and without reserve until he has forgotten the reason for his unhappiness.

Skander watches his distraught, defeated, devastated prey. He feels immense satisfaction. He really had been prepared for greater resistance. He expected to have to use tricks and arguments, to have to implore, threaten, and exhaust his arsenal before getting through to the man. And there he is, falling apart all by himself, baring his neck to the knife, guiding the executioner's hand. It is a total success, even if on some level he misses the enjoyment that hard-won victories bring.

Skander feels a sensation run through him. It is neither pity nor remorse. It is an emotion that swells the chest, makes him feel like strutting and humming. It is the emotion of the conqueror looking at a group of admirers and feeling himself growing wings. He utters a few short coughs, then takes a long, voluptuous sip from his coffee. He makes a sound with his lips, a kind of erotic sucking noise, and puts the cup back down with a slow, almost absentminded movement.

He addresses Menouar without even looking at him, as if his attention were needed elsewhere for something more important. He speaks to him like the teacher to his pupil, the father to his child: "The town hall will be giving a grand reception on Thursday to honor the inventor Mahfoudh Lemdjad in the presence of a great many notables. So you have four days. You can choose the evening before the reception—at the latest. It is an inestimable service you will be performing for the country. During the struggle for liberation many of our comrades gave their lives. For the true patriot it is never too late, even if the war is over."

Stars That Fall into the Eye

The enthralling swarm in the souk. Menouar's mind was carried off by a crazy whirlwind laying waste to any landmark. So this was the city: a never-ending frenzy, clashing images, sharp noises, overlapping and fusing colors. And he had to wait to be fifteen years old to discover this unfamiliar side of the enlightening and whirling world, far from the gloomy edges of his village embellished or marred by the seasons alone.

For Menouar it was an unsettling and auspicious day. He had been waiting for it for a week, never stopping to think of anything else. He knew that the market he was supposed to go to was not like other markets, for it continued throughout the day rather than just the morning. Besides, it was so far away that the villagers who went there only came home at nightfall. And when, that morning at dawn, Menouar had saddled up to set out on the journey, he felt like a different man; he was aware that something irrevocable had just happened in his life.

Three of them had gone off in the cool of the dawn: Mekki, a married man; Lazhar, a strapping youth of nineteen or twenty; and Menouar. The hills in front of them

*rose and fell like ocean waves. The shrubbery looked like
very dark clouds that had come down right to the ground.
Night was still trailing in the sky, the color of antimony,
diluting the mountains' outlines in its pale ink. From time
to time, the horseshoes made sparks on the stones. The
pouches of Menouar's two companions were loaded with
vegetables and fruit. Lazhar was pulling two splendidly
horned rams along, too, tethered to his saddle. Menouar,
on the other hand, was lightly packed. He had nothing to
sell and was simply going along to get to know the world,
the real one, the one with its roots in the city. He had put
on his black shoes, which were a bit stiff for having been
worn so rarely, a gandoura white as snow, and a tight, em-
broidered jacket that his mother had mysteriously found
in a chest (did she have some warrior ancestor?). One
would have thought Menouar was going to a wedding and
that he was the bridegroom.*

*They entered the city early. But the souk was already a
huge magic theater where people were meeting and crowd-
ing each other. They tied their horses up in a eucalyptus
grove.*

*Menouar was walking ahead, without looking back at
his companions. He was floating on a cloud of whimsy. He
didn't feel the rough leather of his shoes slyly eating into
his skin. He was immersed in a mythical space, and yet, he
felt a bit like an intruder. Something or someone seemed
busily trying to draw him away from there—sounds and*

*images seemed to come from far away, reaching him muf-
fled or already extinguished, as if wrapped in cotton wool.
His senses were being assailed; they were warding off unfamiliar colors, sounds, and sights as best they could.
From time to time he would stop to focus more attentively
on some ornament in a store, fabulous clothes such as he
would never wear, and sumptuously elegant people. These
individuals didn't belong with Menouar's people; they
came from among the foreigners who occupied the country. Menouar knew of the existence of these strangers, but
there was no one like them in his village. Without a doubt,
they needed a minimum of comfort to live. And they settled in specific places, such as this fabulous city.*

*Suddenly Menouar was being pulled along by the
flow of the crowd. He let himself drift. Voices were detach-
ing themselves from the confusion of the reverberating
jumble—some were boasting about their merchandise,
others were discussing quality or price. Certain smells were
making him hungry. Menouar was right in the middle of
the vegetable market, where an eclectic garden was displayed in baskets, on mats, and on the ground and where,
without any order or logic in a jumble of greens, reds, and
yellows, vegetables lay side by side.*

*One stall was particularly crowded. In a chant both
foolish and attractive at the same time, a man was singing
the praises of his merchandise—minuscule stones, pow-
ders, dried plants (and even animals) were cluttering the*

little table. Strong smells wafted up from them, some of which got caught in the throat. The vendor, wearing a tall yellow turban with sequins, sat enthroned like a fairy tale prince above the bizarre pharmacy, churning out a comical little refrain enumerating the miracles each object produced. Menouar was struck especially by the virtues of a powder that would dislodge "the stars that had fallen into one's eyes," by which the vendor meant the opacities in the cornea. He explained that these invading spots, which spoil the majesty of one's gaze, are tiny bits of stars that fall into the eyes of the careless. "Be careful not to stare at the night sky too much," he said before going into detail about the way in which his remedies functioned. The explanations seemed inconceivable to Menouar. He had never given any thought to such blemishes in the eye, having been lucky enough not to suffer from them, but he never would have imagined they were caused by bits of stars. He thought of shooting stars, he thought of the smooth stones, black like charcoal, which people at home told him had fallen from the sky and which they called "fragments of lightning."

At the very moment Menouar was thinking of the sky and everything unusual and distorted in it, a young woman caught his eye. One would have thought one of these incandescent "fragments of lightning" had fallen on him. Had a bewildering fear not held him back, he would have gladly cried out at the touch of this burning to bring solace and expel the emotion that so intimidated him. He didn't want to give himself away lest he provoke some undesirable situation. Inside his chest there was a stampede of rabbits.

Obviously, the young woman didn't have any idea he existed. Would she ever? But this didn't seem to bother Menouar. Perhaps he even preferred it this way. At no time had he asked to be repaid with a look or a smile. He didn't even dream of it. Had that happened, he would have taken to his heels without further ado. The situation suited him perfectly. He could let himself be dazzled without fearing anything in return.

The woman was carrying a basket and going casually from one vendor to another as if she had all the time in the world. Her deep sea-blue eyes were looking at no one. Menouar thought that, besides arrogance, he detected a certain cruelty in them. He actually preferred seeing the young woman from the back. That way he was free to delight in her flowing hair (without running the risk of being caught) that was bound to be fragrant with aromatic flowers, her sensuous hips that made you think of slender canoes, and her beautiful bare calves. Inside his own body, too, Menouar felt the impression of warmth and softness her sumptuous body exuded—to the point where he was feeling stifled, thought he was about to faint as when he was struggling against the suffocating steam in the bathhouse.

How bewitching the body of a strange woman is, he thought. How difficult it must be to possess and enjoy it like a man! It is a pitiless endeavor in which you must surely leave behind all your strength, your purse, your herds and horses, and renounce the tranquillity of spirit and the customs that bind you to your village and the land. Would he ever possess this girl? She was older than he, which was a disadvantage. For now, though, Menouar refused to see any other obstacles. He had decided to stop at this one barrier of age alone—and cling to it. That way he could dream and work things out. He could curse the years without which his life would have taken another turn.

Menouar was ruminating and acting in the most perfect state of madness, forgetting the few purchases he had to make. He was magnetized by the young woman and, like an obsequious dog, kept following her at a distance. But he didn't rebuke himself. An unknown feeling that had to be happiness was master over him. No woman in his village had ever aroused such commotion in him.

Anguish engulfed him—the woman was going to disappear, perhaps a man would come and get her. Menouar felt his legs buckle; he wanted to sit down to catch his breath and gather his strength. His painful premonition was not long in coming—the young woman did, indeed, move on without another look at the vendors. Frantic and with leaping heart, Menouar followed her from afar until she disappeared behind a wrought-iron gate. Fortunately, nobody had spoken to her in the course of her passage. Menouar would have died of jealousy, possibly would have put aside his discretion and wariness, thereby running the risk of bringing misfortune down on his head. He felt like crying, like letting the happiness and agitation accumulated inside him give way noisily so that the entire souk would know of his grand adventure, his rapture, and his drama. He was no longer worried about the consequences. He was ready to die, to pay dearly for a fleeting moment of happiness. His body, having known ecstasy, was prepared to accept its torments.

He wandered as if desperate through the immense city of which, from this moment on, he saw, heard, loved, and feared nothing. Three separate times he went prowling around the wrought-iron gate. Each time he had posted himself some ten yards away, pretending to be busy with something so that passersby wouldn't catch him spying. He wanted the young woman to come out again or simply appear at the window, his desire so strong it hurt his stomach. But his hopes were nothing but a pipe dream. At last he decided to move away from the place that had absorbed the captivating apparition. It took Menouar a very long time to forget the woman who had aroused turmoil in him such as no other woman ever would again. That day in the souk would be like no other days before or after; it would always retain its own colors, its own intoxication, and its own torments.

It was almost evening. The three companions, relieved of what they had brought and loaded up with other objects and food supplies, headed back to their horses. Menouar's horse was tied to a thick eucalyptus root unearthed by erosion. It was neighing frantically when its master approached. Although not in the habit of coddling his horse, Menouar stuck his hand in his saddlebag and pulled out a fistful of peanuts, which he held up to the quivering nostrils. Not used to such treats, the animal first hesitated before sticking out his head and tongue. Then it crunched on the delicacies, swishing its tail and scraping the ground with its hoof.

On the way home, Menouar thought that his life had just stopped in order to take a new direction, all because of a young girl who hadn't even looked at him. A piece of him had departed, but without heartbreak and suffering. An unfamiliar feeling had established itself, and Menouar would never be as he was before. The thing was widening within him like a cleft in which the chrysalis of his childhood was being swallowed up. The deceased part of him commanded him to go into mourning. Menouar would never see the girl again. Yet, he was not saddened. An incomprehensible exaltation, an unaccustomed warmth were coursing through his body, which, at times, could not contain the flood. Vague desires and a kind of wish to be dissolved in nature clashed within him. That evening Menouar lived in communion with things he had never thought about before—the peace of dusk over the fields, the trees that autumn had turned red and brown, the smoke that indicated a mysterious human presence in the evening, the rush of a lark surprised in the shelter it had chosen for the night, or, much higher in the sky, the sovereign flight of a small hawk casting a last look over its realm.

Menouar was quiet but agitated. He couldn't sit still in his saddle. Without realizing it, he was suddenly spurring the horse; the animal took off, leaving Lazhar and Mekki far behind, looking at each other dumbfounded by their young companion's behavior. From time to time, Menouar would listen to the conversation of his elders and hold it against them that they were talking about trivial things while he had just experienced an overwhelming day, as momentous as birth or death.

The land around them was drowsy in the gentle autumn air. It, too, seemed indifferent to Menouar's emotion. But that was only how it appeared, for there were forces at work, confronting each other, and Menouar felt all these tensions and dramas inside his own body. Was he ill or drunk? He had never tasted alcohol, but he knew that drunkenness is a state in which one lost one's reason and all sense of moderation.

Now the night was as impenetrable as if the heavenly dome had caved in. The moon had not yet made its appearance. Like navigation lights on the high seas, the fires of the village could be seen from afar. Through the dark firmament a single star made its way, an incandescent tail trailing behind. What eye will it fall into? wondered Menouar. He was thinking about the healer at the market. Does he also heal this unfamiliar sorrow and desire that girls arouse in you, that simultaneously make you want to dance and die?

Menouar was dozing on his horse. In a final thought he coupled the star that had just gone out with the unknown woman in the market.

The paper lanterns lighting the garden of the town hall are in the national colors. The day has been hot and sticky, and, though not truly refreshing, the evening still brings an appreciable lull, locks of a kind damming the torrents of heat. Clouds of fine dust—a multitude of suspended particles—form into flakes in the halo of lights in which whirling nocturnal insects glide in silent flight.

The tables have been set up outside, as has an impromptu platform between the two trees in the garden. That is where the mayor will soon be giving his speech. For now he is talking with other notables—a high-ranking officer delegated by the military command, the assistant magistrate of Mckli, the leader of the local branch of the Party, a wealthy merchant of Sidi-Mebrouk who is also a deputy—all of them professional inaugurators, rhetoricians, specialists in demagogic abstractions, promising the moon and extracting stamps of approval. They have a great deal on their plate in a young country that is being constructed and needs to prevent its citizens from asking themselves questions by answering those questions for them in advance.

Not far from this first council a less prestigious group is forming, consisting of the secretary-general of the town hall, the director of the bank, the head of the city planning office, and a representative of the youth union, who is some fifty years old.

Mahfoudh Lemdjad, who has come under fire and has been pressured from every angle, is now savoring a restorative interlude. He has been quizzed about his work, his machine, his plans, the universities where he studied, his family's place of origin, and then was left alone as if they had drained him of all secrets and he no longer offered any interest whatsoever. He is so thrilled to be done with the questions that he is not in the least concerned about his present solitude. He isn't even wondering whether he will find someone with whom he might have a real discussion or whether he will spend the rest of the evening bored to tears and ill at ease. There is not a single woman in the garden of the town hall. Mahfoudh's perceptiveness in that regard kept him from bringing Samia.

The atmosphere in the luminous clearing, cut into cubes by the paper lanterns in the dense forest of the night, is certainly very different from the ambience at the Scarab—here there is no friendly wine ringing and pitching inside one's head, no foaming beer's mingled colors of wheat and snow in big welcoming glasses. This is not the euphoric and fraternal atmosphere of alcohol spreading around him. Mahfoudh looks at the rows of tables with their bottles of lemon soda and mineral water. As at every official reception, there is not a drop of alcohol. Short of getting completely drunk, Mahfoudh would like to have felt at least a little cheerful in order to face the masquerade to come without constraint and perhaps even with some humor. He would like to have been slightly intoxicated so as to awaken areas of repressed darkness in him, to discover certain clues lying buried beneath the cloak of proprieties and taboos.

Nobody has come to bother him yet—apparently, he has satisfied the curious once and for all. Besides, they are probably motivated by mere polite interest. The people going into the garden have come to eat first of all and, if they are lucky, to rub shoulders with some influential person.

Suddenly, the human cluster rushing into the lighted part of the garden—as if hiding in the dark might look suspicious—goes into motion, resembling a procession of caterpillars coming up against an obstacle. Something big is about to happen, and those far away from the platform are moving closer. Mahfoudh looks toward the dais and sees the mayor going up the wooden steps.

Silence falls. Obviously, the general attention is

focused on the tables and not on the platform, for otherwise the mayor would not have mounted it by himself—with him would have been the high-ranking officer, the assistant magistrate, and the Party leader. Applause rings out from the audience before the mayor begins to speak. Those applauding are urging him to treat them kindly, to keep his speech short so that after the illusion of words they can finally get to the food.

Although his tie torments his windpipe, the mayor nevertheless communicates in the strong and self-assured voice of a man accustomed to speaking and to official rituals: "In the name of the merciful and compassionate God. We have gathered here this evening as members of one united family in order to celebrate a priceless victory that has been added to the ever-growing list of awards for national achievements. Today it concerns neither politics nor soccer—there are multiple areas where our lucky star shines. Tonight there is a young man among the guests who, through his knowledge, his intelligence, his dedication despite obstacles placed in his way by certain self-centered people who are never concerned with the nation's prestige, a man, I say, who has brought glory to our city by choosing it as the cradle of an invention that honors and aggrandizes us. His name is Mahfoudh Lemdjad, and we shall shortly hear him address a few words to us from this humble platform."

The audience begins to stir; from different directions heads are turning toward Mahfoudh Lemdjad—whether they be people with whom he has not spoken or those who, having just heaped questions upon him, look as if, after partially forgetting about him, they're discovering him anew. The mayor has just given him a more remarkable bearing, a more exciting existence.

The speaker allows the small excitement to pass before he continues: "The interest our leaders have in science and the consideration they show scholars are manifested today by the presence in our midst of a representative from the regional command, the assistant magistrate, and other distinguished personalities whom lack of time prevents me from naming. These men, who waged the war of liberation, are today closely pursuing that other war against ignorance and on behalf of progress in order to bring the country's standards up to those of prosperous nations. We thank them for their kind presence, for the valuable time they are granting us this evening. As for Mr. Mahfoudh Lemdjad, through him we salute the sober and useful young who spend their time not by minding other people's business, by criticizing this or that government decision or action, as has become the fashion these days, but by trying to enrich their fellow men with the fruits of their genius. But let it be known that deterrents were placed in the path of Mr. Lemdjad by a man from whom we did not expect such behavior. As for us, it is not our task to judge others and their actions. We simply congratulate Mr. Lemdjad on his determination, on his courage in the face of adversity, and without further ado I now invite him to the modest platform erected on his behalf so that he may honor us with a few words."

Applause accompanies the mayor as he cautiously descends the wooden steps, surely afraid to miss one and go sprawling on the ground. Mahfoudh once again becomes the focus of everyone's gaze as he moves toward the platform, while the mayor comes toward him and embraces him, a gesture that sets off another round of applause.

Mahfoudh knows he's facing a trying moment. Never in his life has he addressed an official gathering, and he never imagined he might have to do so one day. In his head he has concocted an innocuous little speech, neither extravagant nor cavalier. Nevertheless, the prospect of this moment does not particularly upset him, for he knows that people bombarded with repetitive speeches, prophetic directives, and unrealizable exhortations have quit listening a long time ago; no matter what the tenor of the speech, they simply react in the only way that is expected of them—with applause. Furthermore, he knows that today he is the idol of this same town hall that earlier closed all its doors to him—he can say anything that comes into his head and no one will hold it

against him. In the beginning his audience will attend
out of curiosity, to hear the resonance and flow of his
voice; then they'll bow to his words, letting them slide
over their heads as they think about completely different things and obligingly wait for the time to move on
to truly serious matters.

Mahfoudh speaks in a dispassionate voice that he
wishes were full of humor, but humor is appreciated in
different ways, and he doubts this particular audience
would be especially sensitive to it.

"You surely know that people who are involved in
the work of what is called science and the mind are rarely
asked to speak. As a result, they suffer from atrophy of
the tongue. That is why I shall be very brief in my address to you. Before anything else, I would like to thank
this community that is conferring this honor on me
today. It is a place in which I landed by accident and
where I have known joys and worries, sleepless nights
and exhilarating days. But, in spite of it all, I have grown
attached to this city. And now it is adopting me in turn.
As for my modest machine that is receiving somewhat
excessive homage this evening, I will only mention all
that it owes to others, especially to the women who
are absent from our celebration here tonight, but who
for centuries have labored to weave together, thread by
thread, our well-being, our memory, and our everlasting
symbols. By means of a tool with which they ruined

their eyes and hands and that, now that it has almost disappeared, I have reinvented, I express my wholehearted gratitude to them and return to them an infinitesimal part of the many things they have bestowed on us."

Mahfoudh Lemdjad leaves the platform to the audience's enthusiastic applause, without a doubt grateful to the speaker for having spared them by his brevity. He himself is not displeased with his short presentation. He was a bit grandiloquent, he thinks, but without bordering on the ridiculous. In any event, he has acquitted himself of a debt—he has delivered what was expected of him and deserves to sit down in peace and spend the rest of the evening undisturbed, as anonymity ensures, and without being bothered by brash inquisitors with nothing better to do.

Now there is the cheerful clatter of utensils. The gathering is finally beginning to come to life, talk loudly, and gradually drop the mask of respectability. Four waiters are busy around the five attached tables and, as one dish follows another, a good mood sets in and nature takes back her rights. All the disguises, all the forced forms of deference, all the gesticulations on the platform, all the promises of the moon that political necessity decrees, have been dropped off in the coat room one by one.

Mahfoudh is sitting between the town planner and the bank director. He considers himself lucky not to be next to the loftier dignitaries—the assistant magistrate or the military officer, for example, with whom he surely would have nothing to talk about. They let him eat and dream in peace. Now that the formalities are over, the guileful questioners, who weren't even listening to the answers, no longer feel obliged to probe for information that doesn't interest them in the least. They prefer to keep busy with their plates and talk to people with whom they have something in common.

Mahfoudh is happy just to listen. Those who make the history of Sidi-Mebrouk and its environs are no longer discussing matters of public welfare. The interests of the country and the well-being of their constituents have vanished from their minds. They expose their private faces—fathers not of the people but of their own children, husbands not of the Republic but of their wives, managers not of State finances but of their own possessions, concerned not with their city but with their villas. Mahfoudh overhears an impassioned, detailed, and knowledgeable discussion about the metallic bottle green Peugeot 505 SR, which veterans are to receive one of these days thanks to their import permits (five years ago, it was the metallic olive green Peugeot 504 GRD).

But this kind of dinner—stretching into the night, unenlightened, humanized and corrupted by generous and shimmering wine—does not go on for long. Those who drink lemon soda and fruit juice in public, and reserve fine alcohol and fruity wines for private evenings, soon leave the tables with a profusion of congratulations, bows, promises, reminders of promises not kept, and bid each other farewell in the warm evening air, lit by a big round moon that casts shadows as if it were noon.

Having returned the house keys to Rabah Talbi before going to Heidelberg, Mahfoudh tells himself he would have spent this night in Sidi-Mebrouk, had it been possible for him, even at the risk of disappointing the waiting Samia.

To reward the inventor Mahfoudh Lemdjad, the municipality of Sidi-Mebrouk has included him on the list of beneficiaries from the sale of tracts of land.

Ever since he has been living in this suburb with its fake rural features, he has often dreamed of a real landscape after the rain. The sky would be luminous and fresh with a plump, warmish sun in its center, the road washed of all dust; the clean grass would shimmer like green crystal, and inflamed by the sun's reappearance the lark would burst into praise. It was in such a landscape that he had opened his eyes; it was on such a morning that he had slipped into the beauties and the pitfalls of the world. His mother had pushed him out to the inexorable light, telling him very softly, "Menouar, the time has come for you to meet the splendid and perilous earth."

In all sincerity and without wishing to be dramatic, he feels he has encountered more perils than splendors. But he has no reason to complain—his life could have been even more difficult than it was. His childhood and adolescence were so hard that he never could have imagined a day would come when he could eat his fill, as he has been doing for years, or could rest for an entire day without being forced to it by illness, or dress warmly in the winter. For years he herded sheep, in scorching summers that weighed on his shoulders like a mantle of lead, and in winters that tortured his skin and knotted his muscles, in the magnificence of springtime with its flowers exploding like wounds or multicolored bracelets.

Right now he is thinking about the slender yellow flowers whose stems boys would chew to taste their tangy sap and girls would crush to get at the dye with which to redden their hands like henna. The flowers covered vast expanses as soon as the winter rains came to an end. Lambs were submerged in them up to their necks. The wind traced interminable waves that got lost far in the distance where the hills began, upon which clambered scatterings of shrubs.

Looking at the yellow carpet, rolled out to the horizon, little Menouar's head became an immense throne on which every dream could comfortably sit and each in turn might give orders. His soul would be liberated from affliction and cavort beyond the hills. He was listening to the earth sing. Exquisite music and song. Hardly more elaborate than a swarm of insects or a slithering of snakes. But not infrequently, amidst all the chirping in the bushes, would rise the melodious lament of a bird extolling the pangs of love. Luxuriant, luminous, sap-filled, and enticing, nature was voracious. It begged for a massive amount of seed like a woman stricken with hysteria. Children would often eye the impudent ewe. Flowers quivered like butterflies about to take flight. The young were suffocating under an exciting restlessness. The sunshine flowed in a smooth reflection that outlined the shadow of trees. In the blossoming grass, it brought forth a riot of fragrances and colors, flights of gems and shells.

But the finest of all adventures came when a ewe was about to give birth. Menouar had witnessed this anguishing and exhilarating event many times; he had caressed the recumbent animal, placed his hands on the belly shaking with spasms, and with gentle words encouraged labor. Then a wobbly creature would be forced out, and Menouar would pick it up and put it to the nipple. In the evening he'd take the lamb into his arms, the bleating ewe, no doubt thinking they were taking her newborn away from her, hot on his heels.

Menouar is mulling over fragments of his past against the current of time, like a swimmer being dragged off toward the rapids, thinking of the calm waters he has just left. He bores into his memory to chase away the present with its face and orders like those of Skander Brik. He knows now that he will never go back to his land, to see the dazzling run of the seasons one last time. At the very most, with a bit of luck they'll bury him there. He feels thick humus and old smells rise up to him, entwine him like lianas—decayed leaves, fertilizer on the fields in autumn, fires before working the land, the smell of soil overturned by the plow tracing its first furrow, a kind of living wound.

His land, scorched three out of every four seasons, still experiences torrential rain and excruciating cold; it knows how to exhale the rancid odors of decomposition, humidity, and dampness. Menouar thinks of winter. Of the desire it creates in him to curl up. Return to the shell. Return to the warmth of the womb. The magic of the yellow fire. The lullaby of the rain. The wind's savage games between the dry stone walls. The frost clinging to the naked branches with its thin, shimmering claws. The dreadful snow proclaiming the world is a white rock that bites face and feet. Children would make small forays into the street abandoned to the icy winds—under the hoods of their burnooses the cold chiseling their faces into jackals' profiles. They didn't say much, as if words were eradicated by the cold that guarded the unfailing winter silence, as if the mouth when opened would be exposed to an obscure danger. Animals could no longer go to pasture. Branches of the mastic tree had to be cut and brought to the stable. It was a horrible task—Menouar used to come home with his nose stinging as if pliers had pulled at the skin, and his feet would be as numb as blocks of wood. After throwing his load of branches on the ground, he'd rush over to the fire, but instead of warming him the heat would cause sharp pains in his body. At moments like those he cursed his fate as an only child—if, like his friends, he'd had brothers and sisters not carried off at an early age by death, the task would not have fallen to him more than once a week at most. Still, there were less devastating winters—for days, a fine rain would fall, like tightly woven fabric. Sometimes some timid rays of sunshine would mingle with the trembling threads of rain, two complementary colors on the sky's loom. They called that marriage of light and water the "jackal's wedding."

Menouar Ziada is called back to the present—someone is moving around in the house, clattering utensils. His eyes follow his wife as she passes. A jumble of feelings inside him. Pity? Hate? Love? Words can no longer help him get his bearings. Is that his wife or his mother? He has an impulsive but quickly suppressed desire to take that bundle of bones and dried-up skin, with its characteristic, somewhat bittersweet smell of old but clean people, into his arms.

Desire is a word that has become foreign to him. What he would like most is to stretch out, sleep, and furtively pass from one world into the other—from the hellish world of old age to the blessed world of childhood. He has often heard of people who would fall asleep without any particular discomfort and not wake up the next day; people who'd quietly drink their morning coffee while talking with their family or friends and be struck down by noon; people who'd say their prayers, lie down for a short nap, and perish.

The villagers used to describe paradise or hell with many picturesque details, as if they were talking about the little town on the other side of the mountain. In some way, you'd start preparing for death from adolescence onward. But for Menouar this had never helped to make it familiar or merely acceptable. No doubt, this was because he wasn't at all certain of waking up in the hereafter—especially not in a world better than this one (where life, after all, does not overflow with pleasures!). In the minds of the people around him, everything was conceived of and associated with this worst of all worlds and the better one in the hereafter—our miseries are but a simple test to determine our soul's nobility, our suffering is but a transition toward eternal bliss; God is omnipresent and witness to each of our charitable deeds, each of our failures, each of our adulteries, and each of our cases of diarrhea. For the most part, those people were conscious of the fact that their life was only a tributary of purgatory.

Such was the logic of these generations, amputated and disintegrated by death, these generations who suffered in silence, then submissively and with neither joy nor pain accepted and carried on with the actions survival ordered them to embrace, before it was their turn to join the never-ending line of believers who wait for the gong of the Last Judgment in the antechamber of the hereafter. When someone died and it would rain at the funeral, Menouar's mother used to tell her son that heaven felt pity for this pious person. Without daring to say so to his mother, Menouar thought that hundreds of pious people all over the world were dying every day—something to make one hope there wouldn't be a single sunny day in the year!

A life of hard work and deprivation. A stifled adolescence. Desires deferred or dealt with in shame. Yet, dazzling moments, too, as furtive as they were indelible—a bewitching song would sound every day at dusk from the house where the widow Khadra lived. It was a song that used to pervade the village and all the world's dusk:

> *From the sweltering sun*
> *Spare the valiant worker*
> *Who slaves away far from me.*

For Menouar this trite song opened unsuspected horizons, evoked euphoric mornings, rough voyages yet full of delights, construction sites swarming with laborers. Perhaps the words were highly suggestive. Or perhaps all the magic came from the singer's voice. Menouar associated the song with summer, with trees stiff with heat, with the refrain of cicadas. Did the widow never sing in winter, or was it the "sweltering sun" of the song that was playing tricks on Menouar, reinforcing the idea of the warm season? The song had a smell as well. Sweat? Earth stabbed by rain? Cigarette smoke? Every time he heard Khadra's voice, Menouar felt like closing his eyes, lighting a cigarette, blowing puffs of smoke, for then the song described a strange and handsome young man passing the fountain, a cigarette between his lips.

Marriage followed, discovering woman—the one woman of his life. He's listening to her still making noise in the kitchen; she must be soaping, scrubbing, wiping. Clanging of metal. With wonderment Menouar explored her body, but it has become a shadow, his tenderness a desiccated tree. They pass each other in the house, and, without any particular concern, hear the other walk or cough. Perhaps children would have changed their relationship. Menouar will never know what it means to have children. But how dramatic is that really? Is that so important in life? Don't people really have children so that they can die, slowly being pushed toward the tomb by them? Knowing that one is replaced is not much comfort! In reality, mankind, having established a line on this earth, is more difficult to uproot; because he seeks to cling to his terrestrial ties he is more vulnerable and cowardly in the face of death. Menouar wonders if being sterile isn't a lucky thing. At least all is clear, once and for all. You are sheltered from illusions and prophecies. Sheltered from certain worries, too. If children (male, of course—girls don't count) ensure the lineage, the perpetuation of the name, then one should be concerned not only with having (male) children, but they in turn must have (male) children, who should in turn . . . It is a chain of aberrations from which his providential sterility has spared him. It must be a great sorrow to see that one's son is sterile or hampered by a whole string of daughters, which comes down to the same thing. If he'd had any children perhaps his death would have served a purpose—making those children happy. He remembers the death of his mother, whom he really thought he loved; he remembers the feeling of deliverance, of lightheartedness, of freedom—of happiness almost. A few days after the burial he realized he had not one photograph of his mother, nor did anyone else, and he congratulated himself on that flawless disappearance that left not one sign behind to feed affection, regret, or, quite simply, the memory.

What does the woman, so busy polishing, think of all that? She could have left Menouar and perhaps have been a happy mother. But woman does not procreate out of tenderness or for the joy of motherhood. She procreates not to preserve herself but to preserve the man who subjugates her. She would have had as many children as God and man would have wanted her to have.

It is an oppressive day, breathing heavily under the

anvil of the sun. Outside a cicada complains. Menouar's wife must wonder why her husband is staying home today. True, it is very hot outside. Unless Menouar is sick. But she doesn't ask. She is about to. Words weigh too heavily on her tongue. Better they stay there. She does feel like working today, but her tongue is sluggish and motionless like a drowned man. Pots and pans clang together, make ringing noises, and come sparkling from her hands.

Menouar's thoughts suddenly take him back to the period that changed his destiny and the entire country's. The war. He lived through terrible or unexpected events; on more than one occasion he had a brush with death, he was almost executed by his own people, almost became a hero. But he did profit tangibly—material advantages he would have never dared dream of when he was seventeen or twenty. Eat his fill, live in a clean, warm house, go to sleep without wondering whether he'll eat the next day. He has not been very enterprising or else he would have owned more. Like some of his peers who were no more deserving than he, neither in the resistance nor after the war, he would have owned stores, trucks, and monumental buildings. He took only what they gave him, thanking his good fortune for having pushed him to the right side instead of throwing him to the other one. Indeed, he could have joined the ranks of the occupying army. He humbly recognizes that it was luck alone that made the choice for him (can he speak of a lucky star? a lucky star lights your way throughout life). For he had neither the intuition nor the guts of some who had served in the occupying army and then, at the last minute, with all bets placed, rejoined the national army and entered cities or villages as liberators where, a few months (sometimes only weeks) before they were swaggering around in a different uniform. Nor had Menouar dared beg for proof of having been in combat, as had so many others who had never left home during the war and who today hold various titles that bring them not only respect and sometimes immunity, but material advantages as well—preferential jobs, pensions, planned retirement, permission to import goods that cannot be found inside the country.

A perfect, translucent, almost worrisome silence falls over the house. Only the cicada can be heard. The woman has finished doing the dishes, a time-consuming and meticulous chore.

Menouar Ziada now knows exactly what he is going to do and when. It is all a matter of filling the time (from two o'clock to approximately four) that separates him from his deadline. He would have been glad to leave were it not for the shame it would have imposed on him. Still, Skander Brik promised him that his memory would be redeemed and even honored. Menouar isn't sure if he should have faith in these commitments, all the more so as he will not be able to confirm them. He utters fervent phrases even though he knows that men like Skander are capable of any about-face, any form of deceit.

For a moment his life seems to him as constant and calm as a summer sea, washed clean of all the impediments the years of infirmity and wounds have brought. For fourteen hours, as he waits for the bottom wave that will carry him far away from here, Menouar can swim and splash around at length in the unfathomable water of memory, in the protected shelter of childhood. He can again run through certain luminous landscapes, again enumerate and savor the dreams that energized his life—dreams of glory, dreams of pleasure, dreams of friendship, the always-unrealizable dreams because they run parallel to the stunted course of his life.

He is going to force himself to shoulder, one by one, all the lives he would like to have inhabited but from which his actual and wretched life mercilessly evicted him. He knows that dreams enrich and fertilize the imagination and life itself. He does not approve of the very crude society in which he was born—in it dreams are mistrusted as if they were against nature.

A melodious sign comes as if to stab Menouar. A tit in the neighbor's tree. He has heard it several times before. He is sure it is the same one. Just as he is sure he'll never hear it again. Not tomorrow or the following days. He won't defer his severance from what induces light, the power and bravery of desire, the possibility of the dream.

Traveling is always exhilarating. But the journey he is about to undertake is unlike any other. Sure, he has already encountered that dreadful frontier between darkness and light, between the life force and annihilation, on the day when his own comrades tied him up, when unconscious and almost insane he had waited for the bullet or the blade that would deliver him from cold, hunger, injustice, and shame. Miraculously saved, he never thought it would be his lot to relive such a moment. Still, what he experiences today is different—he is going to die unhurriedly and without violence. He himself will arrange everything; he will make every effort to ensure that the setting is tolerable. He will be the ceremony's officiating priest and the atoning victim. He can comfortably move from one role to the other, from one costume to the other. He can submit and watch, decide and execute all at the same time. For a brief moment he thinks with intense horror that his body is going to rot. He looks at his hands, his chest. But then he tells himself it is of no concern to him. The idea of death suggests no landscape or condition to him whatsoever. It remains closed and compressed.

He again remembers his land. He wants to do a retrospective of his life, review the outstanding moments, but he can't find any order. Too many scenes, desires, and feelings are crowded inside his head, where they bump against each other, mingle, fight to the death to get to the narrow exit. He remains stuck in his childhood. His memory is caught like a trapped bird hopelessly struggling to take flight. He sees one moment of that childhood again.

It was a holiday—it was Eid to be precise, not the minor Eid that marks the end of the month of fasting, but the great Eid of the sacrifice. That kind of holiday is the only truce allowing the villagers one day's temporary peace with misery—their unrelenting enemy. It is the only day when every human being, no matter what his condition may be, can turn his back on servitude and take his slice of joy.

It started at dawn. They would get up in a hurry—often after a sleepless night of anticipation—to inhale the smell that hung in the air, a smell of celebration, blood, and pleasure that knots the stomach. It was a morning like no other. Even before the animals were shackled, people were experiencing a silent elation, immersed in an intense but continuous celebration, waiting for the knife to make the cut . . . Then jubilation would spread in everyone's heart, rumbling like a storm.

The one to cut the animals' throats was not just anyone: he had tact and prestige; devotion and know-how had to dwell together in him. He showed himself to be obliging and patient, but was thereby no less aware of his own importance. This could be seen in the superior attitude he flaunted to look those up and down who brought him their rams, in the condescending and protective attitude he adopted with the children around him (he never chased them away; you sensed that he needed spectators). Yet, it wasn't exactly a big affair. A simple ritual act, as impersonal as it was instantaneous. He would take the knife red with the blood of the previous sheep, softly utter a phrase, and the blade would move from one ear to the other. Then the man would let go of the jugular vein he had been pressing with his left hand and jump aside in order not to be splashed with the blood that spurted far and wide. When he, the vanquishing god of this battlefield where some fifteen animals lay dead, had finished everything, he wiped his knife on the grass, then dropped it in a pail of water and left it there. He washed his hands and hairy forearms thoroughly in another bucket.

The animals were suspended, head down, from the branches of ash or olive trees. Knives and axes were put to work; organs and offal would fall into the dishes with a soft thud. There would be a great deal of meat in the soot-blackened pots that evening. The children had watched the struggle from a distance, seen the animals struck down in a concert of bleating. The men at work, whom they were bothering, sometimes chased them gruffly or with a deceptively threatening gesture. But they'd come back like a swarm of flies, for they were waiting for the moment when the bladders would be pulled out and thrown away, then grab them to empty and inflate them. It was not unusual for a hunched-over old woman to approach a dying animal and collect its still-streaming blood in an earthenware vessel. To what purpose? One day, in a dark corner of the house among small bins of seed and two huge black cauldrons used only for celebrations, Menouar had discovered a vessel like this (perhaps an emaciated old woman had left it there or else his mother, too, was involved in these dubious practices). The blood had hardened and turned black and the upper layer was cracked, making him think of eczema scabs.

The Eid he suddenly remembers is a specific one, spoiled by a little girl's desperate tears. The shepherdess Yamna was being dragged along the ground, hanging on to an eighteen-month-old lamb going to slaughter. She was wailing, begging them to spare this lamb, which she had raised and cherished like a family member. Her father, who must have thought Yamna was going beyond the limits of the ridiculous and disturbing the sacred joy of this day, began to kick and punch her to make her let go. Since she was resisting and screaming, her father's rage increased. He started beating her blindly, and the little girl's blood was already blending with that of the slain animals on the ground before people intervened and pulled her away from him. Little Menouar, whose heart was quick to tremble and be touched (he knew it wasn't the same for every child), felt a curtain had fallen over the celebration. In any event, he knew the party was over for him. That evening he couldn't touch his dinner of tasty meat and wouldn't for another year around the same time.

Menouar eats his lunch like a robot, rather fast and without paying it any particular attention. He doesn't know if he was hungry while eating and is now satisfied. The sun has dwindled. The air coming into the house is tepid afternoon air. The light, too, is less abrasive. How much time can be spent just in remembering!

Menouar's mind is numb, his limbs heavy. He feels as if he's about to fall asleep—to know at last that state of grace where he can escape from himself, his miseries, his grudges, and his ghosts. But he doesn't fall asleep. He is dozing, eyes closed so as to be better cut off from the present. The muezzin starts his melodious and moving call, both soothing and grating at the same time. Is the paradise religion promises as sweet and musical as this chant? Although the muezzin has been silent for a few moments, it still seems as if his echo continues like a timeless expression, like a restful and delicious breath seeking to fuse with the peace of dusk. Menouar would like to move, but he can't. He doesn't know whether it's his mind not speaking loudly enough to his limbs or whether these have grown treacherously stiff. He is like the folk tale character being devoured by a monster (an ogre?) that starts at his feet, moving progressively up to his head, which continues to think and speak. He drifts among the earthy smells and gentle lights of a fleeting, bygone, inaccessible region . . .

The hour of the swifts has arrived. Their feverish and silky flight. Menouar feels the light fade; night is moving in fast. He doesn't need to go out to know that the sun, no longer visible, is shooting a large reddening beam at the sky, like the enchanting tail of a peacock. The world can now rest, prepare fresh mysteries, and renew its spent energies to face the next day's race. God's weakest creatures, the insects put off by the sun and the day's glow, can now enforce their presence. They'll begin to make noise, sing, coo, and get carried away for the parade of love. Menouar would like to have antennae grow, just like theirs, elytrons singing like lyres, a hard shell. He would have lived far from the decrees of men in the coolness of the underbrush, the moving branches of shrubs, rolled up under a stone, waiting for the right hour or season. When insects disappear do they also go to heaven? Perhaps it is appropriate to first be sure that humans, indeed, have theirs. If heaven exists, it must be shaped like a cozy nest on a leafy branch beyond the reach of predators; it should have the consistency of a padded burrow where you doze while the world above carries on. He is almost certain that heaven is not what those fanatic, hot-tempered, and intolerant preachers hold out, those who never hesitate to invoke violence, who take the saber as their emblem, exclude instead of embrace, condemn instead of absolve.

Menouar has no appetite. He has come to the table for dinner, but his jaws are locked, his stomach turns at the sight of the food. He spends a long time washing up as if grooming for the mortuary; then he lies down on the bed to continue his daydreaming. He knows he will not sleep. And he doesn't sleep even for a minute. He gets up several times and looks at his alarm clock. It seems to be dragging like an exhausted runner. The hands move forward regretfully as if they, too, were going toward their death. One-ten, two-thirty-eight, four-twelve, five-oh-nine. Menouar Ziada gets up. It is the morning call to prayer. Soon the view will be a long line of chattering birds that dawn revives and makes sing each morning.

The rope has been carefully knotted. Menouar climbs up on the chair without trembling. He never thought he'd have this much determination, this much courage. His mind is free, clear, and quick in a way he didn't think possible. He barely feels his blood pulse slightly faster through his body. He waits patiently, absolved of every impurity and every degrading cut. Yes, he waits with majestic calm for the inescapable. It will be orderly, relentless, and kind.

The rope around his neck, he leans first forward then backward in almost grotesque movements. His foot knocks the chair over. But he can't fling it as far as he had wished. He feels something tear apart. A snake coils around him, prevents his blood from circulating. A massive scaly beast has chosen to live in his throat, decided to stay there until he has choked. A torrent of pain pulls at him where he struggles. He gathers all his forces, focuses and hardens them to launch them against this agony. But the stranglehold of suffering tightens, its millstone weighing down on the conquered and shattered body. For a second or two, Menouar hopes it is a dream from which he will soon awaken, as he used to wake up as a child the moment he was about to come tumbling down from a mountaintop.

Menouar knows a village. A tangle of alleyways runs through it. They link the things of this world and the things of worlds foretold—the silted river, the stars that guide lost souls, the birds mistreated by winter, the ogre hiding in the dark, the tree of heaven whose shade a galloping horse cannot manage to outrun, the cemetery on the edge of the village connected to it by an underground passage—and those who know the formula can have dialogues there with the dead! In this underground passage Menouar . . .

The novelist, poet, and journalist **Tahar Djaout** was shot by assassins outside his home in Bainem, Algeria, on May 26, 1993. He died on June 2 after lying in a coma for a week. Djaout's murder was attributed to the Islamic Salvation Front; one of his attackers stated that he was killed because he "wielded a fearsome pen that could have an effect on Islamic sectors." Author of eleven books of poetry and fiction, including *Les Vigiles* (winner of the Prix Méditerranée), Djaout was considered one of the most promising writers of his generation.

Marjolijn de Jager is an award-winning translator who is known for her work with Francophone literature. She currently teaches courses in literary translation at New York University.